Under My Skin

Under my skin

Gail Vinall

Scripture Union

Copyright © Gail Vinall 1997
First published 1997

Scripture Union, 207–209 Queensway, Bletchley,
Milton Keynes, MK2 2EB, England.

ISBN 1 85999 018 5

British Library Cataloguing-in-Publication Data.
A catalogue record of this book is available from the British
Library.

Printed and bound in Great Britain by Cox & Wyman Ltd,
Reading.

For Mum

1

Mr Campbell put the final mark in the register and looked up. A quick glance over the tutor group to check uniform resulted in the usual raised eyebrow at Scott. The rest of the group grinned.

'Mum says my top's still in the wash, Sir, and I can't have new shoes until her cheque comes in…'

'Yes, all right Scott, just keep out of Mr Staines' way.' 9C liked Campbell. He was no walk-over but he wasn't on your back all the time, not like Staines, the Headmaster. Campbell was one of the youngest teachers at Milbain Comprehensive and had only arrived in September, but he was pretty popular already.

There was a general surge towards the door as the bell sounded for the end of morning registration. Campbell waved them on and then remembered.

'Hang on, 9C – one more thing – new boy starting today. His name is Anthony, from Birmingham, and he'll be in your period 1. Make him welcome.

Right, off you go.'

'I hope he's dishy,' said Karen Schofield, as they lined up for Science. 'It's time we had a bit of talent in this tutor group.' She pouted disparagingly at the group of boys lounging against the radiator behind her.

'What's wrong with me?' Alan Ackford said, striking his Wolfman pose.

Karen giggled and gave him a light punch on the arm. All the boys fancied Karen but she was into year 10 boys.

'Well, I hope he's a decent footballer,' Paul said.

'Too right,' Kevin agreed. 'We might not get hammered by 9S for a change.'

'You'd need more than one decent player to make any...'

'9C line up.'

'Oh no, it's Staines,' Scott groaned, 'Reeder must be off sick again.'

'Quite right, Scott Levin, Mr Reeder is sick, just as I am sick of seeing you out of uniform, however not so sick that I cannot endure your presence in my after-school detention tomorrow.'

'But Sir...'

'Tomorrow!' Staines' booming voice echoed around the lab and the word hung in the air. You could almost see the exclamation mark hanging over the teacher's bench.

A timid tap at the door broke the atmosphere. The school secretary poked her neat perm around the glass pane.

'New boy for 9C, Headmaster.'

Staines' faced beamed. He assumed a jolly smile and looked as if he might be about to bring out the *Werther's Originals*.

'Anthony Ahmed,' the secretary piped and then disappeared. 9C did a collective double take.

Anthony Ahmed might have been a terrific footballer, might have been the sexiest male Karen had ever clapped eyes on, but what he was, unquestionably, was black. The only black kid at Milbain. Everyone in the room gawped, except for Staines. All Staines could see, Paul reflected with some admiration, was the perfect uniform, the buffed shoes, the creased trousers. Staines' chest expanded as he beckoned Anthony in and personally ushered him to an empty seat.

'Now 9C, the introductions are over. Let us begin. Turn to page 41. Resistance.'

It was lunch time before anybody could discuss the new kid, but it wasn't long before the typical sick jokes began. Paul felt uncomfortable hearing his friends coming out with all the usual rubbish.

'Where's Ahmed gone?'

'Checking out the canteen — they've got a new arrival of bananas.'

'What's next?'

'Gym.'

'Ahmed'll be up those ropes like lightning!'

'Anyone playing football?' Paul bounced the ball enticingly but, for once, received little response. Kevin, Scott and Alan continued their barrage of abusive comments. Even Karen was holding court, discussing what her dad would do if she ever brought home a black bloke.

Paul stayed out of the conversation, awkwardly dabbing the ball with his toe.

'What's the matter with you?' Alan demanded, his

blue eyes narrowing.

Paul shrugged. 'Nothing!'

'What do you think of him, then?'

'We don't know him – no one's spoken to him yet.'

'I'm not having a jungle bunny as a mate!'

Paul squirmed but felt obliged to snigger. Alan was his best mate. It had taken him long enough to settle into Secondary School; he didn't feel like falling out over a total stranger. Anyway, Anthony was bound to find his feet and get some friends in a couple of days. There was no need for Paul to get involved. Even so, he was glad when the bell went for PE. Mr Parr was almost as strict as Staines and wouldn't stand for any nonsense. The snide comments subsided as soon as they entered the changing rooms.

Anthony changed on his own. Paul glanced at him a few times. His kit, like his uniform, was brand-new. His parents must be well-off. At any rate they had made sure he had everything he could possibly need for Milbain. Perhaps Paul ought to say something. He knew all too well how it felt to be on your own. Just then Anthony looked at him. Paul blushed because he had been staring. The words froze in his mouth and he only managed a stiff little nod. The new boy looked puzzled and then smiled a bit but Paul kept a half-eye on Alan and followed him out before Anthony could catch up.

It was football, Paul's favourite lesson, but the game wasn't any good. Despite Paul's hopes, the new kid wasn't a footballer. Even when he had the ball, which wasn't often because no one passed to him, he fluffed simple passes. He was quite tall but gangly and rather uncoordinated. 9S quickly took the lead and forged ahead. They played as a team and knew where their players were. 9C were in disarray. Alan flatly refused to acknowledge that the new kid was on the pitch. Paul tried to pass the ball to Anthony who either missed it or, on one occasion, ended up being tackled by his own side. He was a disaster. Mr Parr yelled and whistled from the sideline, finally stopping the game and ordering dribbling practice in pairs. Anthony, of course, ended up without a partner and had to play with the teacher. It was a frustrating and irritating game which left everyone in a sour mood.

Paul was glad when home time came, and he felt sufficiently fed up with Alan and Kevin to make excuses about having to be home early so he didn't have to hang around with them. He'd heard enough stupid jokes to last a lifetime. Paul was also angry with himself for always being worried about what Alan thought of him. He liked him a lot; he especially liked being part of Alan's gang – it was safe and strong. Nobody gave you any trouble if you were with Alan. On the other hand if you happened to disagree with Alan, or anything he did, it was best to keep your mouth shut. That was all right usually but the way he was treating this new kid was wrong. So why didn't Paul have enough guts to say something?

He thrust his hands in his pockets and kicked a stone. It spun, ricocheted off a fence and caught him on the shin. Paul scowled and shook his blonde fringe out of his eyes. He hadn't showered after football and the dried sweat itched between his shoulder blades.

When he arrived home, Paul's mother was in the kitchen unpacking groceries. He wandered through to give her a hand and grab a few snacks at the same time.

'Good day, love?' Mrs Evett paused as she stooped

to the fridge to glance up at him. She wrinkled her nose, smiling.

'I know, I need a shower,' he grunted.

'Not a good day!' his mum answered her own question.

'There's a new boy!' He hadn't meant to say anything but it sort of just blurted out.

'Oh, do you like him?'

Paul shrugged, 'Haven't spoken to him.'

'Why not?'

'Alan doesn't like him.'

'And you have to follow Alan?' His mum's tone became sharper.

'No.' Yes, actually.

'Why doesn't Alan like him?'

'I don't know.' Because he's black. The unspoken words echoed in Paul's brain. Was it as simple as that for Alan? Did he feel that way too?

'You'd better take that shower.' It was a dismissal.

Paul left the kitchen reluctantly. His mum never shouted at him and rarely moaned but she had a way of putting a distance between herself and other people when she disapproved of something. His mum would have talked to the new kid, just as she always spoke to new people at church when they went there on Sunday mornings. Dad warmed up later, once he really knew the people, but Mum was brilliant at starting up conversations, smiling and listening so that any awkwardness was smoothed away. She'd talk to anyone – people in shops, on the bus, even in waiting-rooms.

Paul felt the hot needles of water drilling into his back, washing away the sweat and irritation of the day. He stuck his head under the shower-head and then shook himself like a dog so that the hair stood out in a halo of spikes. Emerging from the steamy bathroom, Paul sniffed at gammon steaks and chips – his favourite – and squeezed the confused thoughts about Alan and Anthony firmly to the back of his mind.

They could be dealt with later.

The next morning brought the problem back into focus as soon as Paul entered his tutor room for registration. The new boy was sitting at a desk alone and there was a semicircle of empty space around him as obvious as if it had been painted on the classroom floor. Paul glanced nervously over to his group of friends and, seeing that they weren't looking in his direction, gave the boy the briefest of nods. The boy saw but gave no response. Paul despised himself for his cowardice, for caring so much about what Alan thought, for wanting to be like the gang. Just like the shoes.

Last month he'd whined on and on about having a pair of Kickers. Ordinary moccasins wouldn't do, nor the cheaper alternatives. They had to have the Kicker label. After days of sulking and persuading, Dad had taken him out to buy them. He'd been so happy, so grateful but really more than anything else he'd been pleased because it kept him like the gang. Alan had Kickers, so he must have some too. To be honest, he wasn't wild about them personally, in fact they'd rubbed a nasty blister on his heel in the first week, but he'd gone on wearing them, being really nonchalant when other kids noticed them. It was pathetic when you came to think about it. And it never stopped, because this week Alan had come in with a 'Slammin Vynal' coat. There was no chance his parents would ever let him have one of those but he'd still have to try to change their minds. It shouldn't matter what you wore or what you looked like, Paul reflected as he joined the gang. Alan clapped him on the back and Kevin offered him half a piece of chewing-gum. It was good to have friends to be able to join in. But if they were real friends, why was he worried about things like shoes and having the right bag?

He stole a quick glance at Anthony who was trying to pretend he was interested in the health poster on the wall. It suddenly struck Paul that all the designer labels in the world couldn't help Anthony. He was just the wrong colour. He couldn't buy friends.

Campbell strode into the room with his jacket flying open. He had a natty line in ties. Today's was garish green, and made up, if you looked closely, of lines of frogs, mouths open, toes spread. He gave the impression of being very disorganised but as he raked the classroom it was obvious that he was taking note of the absentees, the uniform, the friendship groups and Anthony, painfully alone.

Paul sat down beside Alan, their elbows just touching. He didn't notice Campbell's eyes on him and the thoughtful pouting of the lips as the teacher's eyes swept back to Anthony. Paul was laughing at some daft exploit of Alan's when Campbell's voice cut into their conversation.

'Ah Paul, I'd like you to be responsible for going round with Anthony today – perhaps you'd like to come and sit next to him now and get acquainted.'

It wasn't an invitation. Paul flushed and momentarily hated Campbell for doing this to him. Fortunately, Alan gave him a pitying look and Kevin only smirked, so Paul picked his bag up reluctantly and made his way to the front desk as if he were a gladiator approaching the wild lions – a tragic yet heroic figure. In a way Paul felt relieved. Now at least he could have a clear conscience as far as talking to the new kid went and, into the bargain, keep his street cred with Alan and the others. After all, he hadn't chosen to be with the new kid, he'd been forced.

'Dump him by break,' Alan whispered, loud enough for Anthony to hear as he passed their desk on the way out. Paul mumbled something, embarrassed, but Anthony just got up and strode off ahead of him.

'Hang on,' Paul said.

'It's all right, I know the way. I don't need a minder and I'm not a charity case.'

Paul felt a wave of shame for his friends. He determinedly kept up with Anthony and sat next to him in English despite the stony silence. Eventually the stranger relented and between the reading of Romeo and Juliet Act 3, Paul had established some idea of where he'd lived in Birmingham, what his dad did, the fact that he had no brothers or sisters, like Paul, and that they'd moved into a house just up the hill from Paul. Anthony was a useful person to sit next to, having a wide array of pens, coloured felts and Maths equipment. At this stage in the second term, Paul had lost or lent most of his. Anthony was very open-handed with his property and how could Paul refuse his chewing-gum at break time without appearing rude?

He purposely took him on a tour of the school at break to avoid the playground and Alan. They ran into Campbell instead.

'I've got you a locker key, Anthony. Show him where H506 is Paul, then he needn't lug that bag around all day.'

'Look I can find my own locker, it's okay. Your mates will be waiting.'

'It's all right – we've got Tech before lunch and you'll never find it on your own. I can see them at lunch.'

Paul would have liked to have ditched Anthony there and then but he couldn't. Alan would just have to wait. Anyway, they were in different technology groups so Paul could just say he'd been looking for him.

As they passed the computer suite at the junction with the locker area, Anthony's wide brown eyes lit up.

'Hey, can we use the computers out of class?'

'Sure. There's a club I think, most lunch times. Ask Mr Dobbs. You keen on computers then?'

'Yeah. I'm going to be a programmer like my dad when I leave university.'

'We haven't even chosen options for GCSE yet.'

'I have. Dad sorted it out with Staines when we came to look around. That's why we chose Milbain.'

His tone made Paul think that Anthony had plenty of doubts about Milbain now that he'd arrived. He felt embarrassed again.

'What was your old school like?'

'Friendlier,' Anthony replied, looking him straight in the eye.

'I can imagine,' Paul murmured.

'Look, it's been really good of you, sticking with me today but you needn't bother. I like being on my own.'

'Liar.'

Anthony laughed, the dazzling creamy teeth flashed. He had a great face for pulling all kinds of expressions and when he was being serious, a strong, dignified kind of look. Paul had to look up to Anthony slightly, as he was shorter. At first it had made him feel even more insignificant, like a pale shadow of the other boy, but at the same time he liked being the leader, the one in charge. Usually Paul was dragged around at Alan's elbow, doing things his way.

Paul didn't like food technology much but with Anthony it was different. They were making bread and Anthony kept using their dough as a punch bag or spinning it around his head like a pizza. In the end though, Mrs Williams proclaimed their loaf to have the best texture and flavour in the class. Paul was revising his opinion of the new kid and when the final bell went he found himself walking home with Anthony.

It was only when he said bye to Anthony that he remembered Alan, and the fact that they usually played extra football on a Wednesday. He'd have some grovelling to do the next day to get back into Alan's good books. But maybe they could all be friends together. They weren't like a group of girls who fell out whenever anyone new tried to nestle in. Surely once Kevin and Alan realised what a good bloke Anthony was, they'd accept him as a mate. He wasn't any different when you came down to it.

The next morning at school these fanciful hopes were dashed as soon as Paul entered the gates. Alan was waiting, hands on his hips, his friends around him. Paul saw them first and bounced over, trying to be nonchalant.

'Watcha,' he called.

Alan sneered at him. 'Finished baby-sitting?'

Paul shrugged. 'It was only Mr Campbell…'

'I said ditch him at break.'

'Yeah well, Campbell got him a locker and I ...'

'We know.' There was a sinister titter which rippled around the gang.

'H506.' Kev giggled.

'So what?' Paul knew there was something up, but he couldn't work out what. His heart hammered uncomfortably. It was ridiculous – these were his mates but he was an outsider. In fact, he was worse off than Anthony, caught in the middle so he couldn't be friends with anybody.

'What have you done?' he asked, trying to veil the accusation in his voice.

'Nothing,' Alan replied, silky smooth like the adder's tongue!

'Listen, why can't we all get along with him? He's okay really – you'd like him.'

'Forget it. Are you with us ... or not?' Alan glared at Paul, his blue eyes glowering with anger. Paul was defeated. He couldn't defend Anthony against them and he couldn't stop wanting to be part of their close gang. It was all very well for Campbell. He was an adult. He could make up his own mind. It wasn't the same for people like Paul, on the outside of groups, trying to be a part of something.

He shuffled closer to the gang who spread out to let him in like some gigantic Venus fly trap.

As they entered the classroom for registration as one body, Paul kept his eyes on his shoes. He didn't want to see Anthony's lonely figure nor the disdain in Campbell's face. Something had happened, he could feel it. A group of girls watched them as they entered and gave each other a series of nudges.

'Perhaps you likely lads can give us some help. Alan

18

'Perhaps you likely lads can give us some help. Alan Ackford – we are missing a school bag – any ideas?' Campbell was angry.

'Me Sir? No Sir.' Alan piped innocently.

Paul knew now what they were up to. It must be Anthony's bag and it must be out on the ledge just below the window, out of view unless you leant out. If Campbell had been here a bit longer he'd have known. It was one of the oldest tricks in the book. Everyone's bag ended up on the ledge at some point in their first term. Within reach if they were just ordinary, out of reach if they were a victim and straight out of the window if they were a complete dork.

The only boy not to have had his bag on the ledge had been a wimp called Marvin, whom everyone felt sorry for because he was a bit lame on one side and it would have been too mean for anyone to do it to him. In the end he threw his own bag out of the window just to fit in and the whole class had a lunch time detention because their naive class teacher in Year 7 hadn't believed even Marvin could be that dumb. After that Marvin's bag lived pretty well permanently on the ledge and Marvin was as happy as a pig in muck while it lasted.

'Try again, Alan,' Campbell hissed, 'or shall we sit here until you remember?'

Paul squirmed in his seat. He wanted to say something but Alan's elbow in his side was hard and bony. He glanced at Anthony standing beside Campbell and felt like a traitor. Seconds became minutes.

'Oh for goodness' sake, I'm not sitting here for you load of idiots,' Karen suddenly burst out. 'It'll be on the ledge, Sir.'

fetch it, Alan?'

'I didn't put it out there,' Alan said.

Teacher and boy faced each other in combat. Campbell had never been tested before but Paul could tell, from the twitch in the muscle at his jaw, that he wasn't going to give in on this one.

'Fetch it, Ackford.'

Alan hesitated and then decided not to push it. He didn't have an argument with Campbell, but with the new kid and he'd made his point there.

Campbell dismissed them curtly. As Karen passed Alan he whispered something abusive but she flounced past, unconcerned. Karen had too many friends in the upper school to bother with Alan's silly threats, and he knew it.

'Push off, Ackford,' she said. 'You and your lap-dogs. You're pathetic, all of you.'

Paul followed behind Alan, feeling the sting of the girl's words. It came to something when it took a girl to face up to Alan. At the door, Campbell called him back.

'Thanks for looking after Anthony yesterday.'

'It was nothing, Sir.'

'Well, I'm sure it meant a lot to him, and I thought you two looked as if you'd got a lot in common yesterday.'

'Yes, Sir.' Paul shuffled uncomfortably. He could see where this was leading.

'Have you been friends with Alan for a long time?'

'About a year, Sir.'

'I see, well, of course old friendships matter, but as you grow up – well, people can change.'

Paul stood looking aimlessly around.

'Do you want me to go round with Anthony again?'

'No, Paul. That's your decision. He's big enough to look after himself. Anyway, Alan wouldn't let you introduce Anthony into his gang would he?'

'No Sir, well, Anthony's not Alan's type.' It sounded feeble even as he said it.

'Don't you mean Anthony is black?'

Paul looked up, shocked. Teachers weren't supposed to say such things, not right out like that.

'Let's be honest, Paul. We may not be able to do anything about it but let's not avoid the truth, eh?'

Paul looked into Campbell's solemn face and wished he didn't feel as if the teacher was disappointed in him.

'Still go to St Lawrence's Church, Paul?'

'Yes Sir, Mum and Dad go, and I go with them.'

'And the youth club?'

'Not any more. I go to football with Alan and the others – it's the same night.'

'You like your football, don't you?'

'Love it, Sir. Do you go then, to church, Sir?'

'Yes, Paul. St Mark's. It's nearer to where I live. I met your mum at a joint service last month.'

Paul nodded. Of course, it would be Mum. He wanted to make things right.

'I'm sorry about the bag, Sir. Alan would have only meant it as a joke.'

'I know. The thing is, jokes can get out of hand. You have to know where to draw the line.'

'Yes, Sir.' Paul stood confused. He had a feeling Campbell wasn't just talking about Alan.

'Well, off you go – don't be late for first lesson.'

Despite hurrying, Paul was a minute late for Maths and could only escape the teacher's notice and recriminations by sitting just inside the door while he

21

was giving out text books at the back of the room, where Paul normally sat with Alan. Anthony was sitting next to a girl in glasses directly in front of the teacher's desk.

From his vantage point Paul watched Alan, taking secretive little glances unnoticed by the gang. He knew more plans were afoot from the way they passed knowing glances and from the fact that first Alan and then Scott asked permission, and were granted it, to visit the loos. Suddenly Paul knew it had something to do with the lockers and, in particular, H506. He also knew that he couldn't sit back and watch it any more.

'Please Sir, can I be excused?'

'Another one! Has the whole class suddenly become incontinent?'

'It's urgent, Sir.'

'Very well, but be quick.'

Outside of the classroom, Paul scooted to the locker area knowing what he would see, yet still hoping he was wrong. H506 was on the bottom row. Neatly arranged on the floor was a banana skin like a lemon glove with the fingers splayed. The creamy mush had been squelched into the lock and, daubed over the metal door in thick felt pen, were racist jibes in six inch high letters. Anger welling from Paul's stomach had a calming effect. He picked up the banana skin and binned it then ran to the loos for wet paper towels. Thankfully the pen wasn't indelible. He rubbed at the letters, smearing red ink all over the door, and scooped up as much of the banana flesh as he could. There wasn't time to do a proper job but the worst was gone by the time he got back to the lesson.

As he returned to his seat, Alan's eyes were like a

hawk's: beady, detached, all-knowing. Their eyes met and Paul would not drop his gaze. Alan looked momentarily surprised, then his eyes hardened like icy rocks. Well, that was it, then. War was declared. Anthony, oblivious to the drama of which he was at the heart, packed his bag as the bell sounded for break. Paul waited for him outside the Maths room and steered him in the direction of the canteen. He hadn't particularly wanted to be his friend but now it looked as if Anthony might end up his only friend. There again, if Alan was capable of that kind of sickening thing, maybe Paul was better off without him.

2

Over the next few days, it seemed to Paul that all Alan's proclaimed hatred for the new kid had been transferred almost exclusively onto him. He had expected to be an outcast as far as the gang was concerned, was resigned to Alan's jibes and taunts about being in love with his coloured cousin etc but what had surprised and upset him were Alan's personal attacks.

It had started with the horrible verbal battle about the locker incident which had happened that day after school by the bike sheds. Alan, beside himself with rage, had called Paul every disgusting name he could think of. Paul had taken it without flinching although he had been tempted to doff him one on the nose once or twice, despite his hatred of violence, especially when Alan had called him a snivelling coward which Paul thought a bit rich considering the trouble he'd kept Alan out of. Campbell would have gone ballistic if he'd had wind of what Alan had done, which he certainly would have sooner or later.

'You ought to be grateful to me! You're such a prat, you never know when to stop,' Paul had hurled back.

'It was nothing to do with you.'

'Yes it was. Everybody's got something to do with that kind of thing. It was well out of order and you know it.'

Actually, Paul had got the impression that Kevin, Scott and the rest weren't really behind Alan. They were with him, just as they always were, but not egging him on. They had just mooched around not saying much. Maybe that was why it hadn't ended up with Paul getting a thump. He'd resigned himself to getting a beating and when it didn't happen felt mildly irritated that he hadn't stood up to Alan before.

Not sure how to intimidate his former friend, Alan resorted to the small but hurtful humiliations which proved to Paul once and for all that he had never been a friend at all. Secrets they had confided and confidences shared were common property. The fact that Paul went to church with his parents had never interested Alan before, but now it was a thing constantly referred to as proof of what a wet Paul was. He and Campbell became the 'God squad' of the tutor group and while Campbell smiled serenely and was quite unfazed, Paul hated it.

It was horrible being different. He even considered stopping going to church but he couldn't face telling his parents that he wasn't going with them. It wouldn't make things any better between him and Alan anyway.

At school, Paul stuck with Anthony, not because he really wanted to but because now he was determined to make a point of it. Campbell smiled and nodded at him but his teacher's approval didn't make up for the loss of his entire social life.

Paul stopped going to the football practice on Tuesday evenings. He'd tried to go once but Alan had made it so pointed that he wasn't welcome that all the fun of the game was lost. Instead, Paul took to disappearing upstairs to his room every evening, despite the fact that towards the end of April the weather started to acknowledge that it might be edging towards summer.

Paul's parents didn't pry but they realised what the falling out had been about.

'You know you shouldn't sit at that computer every evening,' Mum complained, passing his bedroom shortly after supper.

'Why not?' Paul kept his eyes on the 'Shoot 'em up' game.

'You'll get retina burn from those stupid flashing lights.'

'Well there's nothing else to do.'

'We're walking down to the canal later. Want to come?' Mum offered. The airing cupboard was in Paul's room and she was stacking clean towels in neat piles around the tank.

Paul bit back the disparaging reply. His mother tried to be nice but sometimes she was clueless. She didn't realise that fourteen-year-olds didn't go walkies with their parents. They could bump into all kinds of kids down at the canal. He didn't need any more fuel for the playground comments. Paul could just imagine it. 'Saw you last night. Daddy taking you to sail your boat was he?' That was another part of the designer label syndrome. Parents were uncool. Paul was very fond of both of his but what with his mother's capacity for unprovoked conversation and his father's recent attachment to khaki-coloured shorts and, horror of horrors, sandals, it was becoming well-nigh impossible to be seen anywhere with them.

Paul's mum finished stacking towels and came to stand behind him. It put Paul off and he lost two lives almost immediately. She didn't seem to notice.

'Well if you won't walk with us, why not cycle round to Anthony's house. He seemed a nice lad when you brought him in the other day after school. You could invite him to football practice.'

'I've given up football.'

'What! You love football.'

'I prefer computers.'

'I don't believe it! Hey, Brian, can you believe it? Paul says he's given up football!'

Paul crashed himself into the alien landscape and switched to re-load. As his dad joined them he pushed stand-by. It looked like he was in for some quality time. Considering how many times his mum had complained about broken plants as a result of his dribbling practice in the back garden you'd have thought she'd be pleased he was into something more garden-friendly. But oh no – they were having a debriefing session now.

'Football's better for you than all this tripe,' his dad was saying.

'Dad, those disks were in order.'

'Oh, sorry old chap. Shouldn't these be in their cases?'

'I was going to play them in a minute – while you're out on your walk,' Paul added, just in case they'd forgotten. He hoped his mum might take the hint and leave him in peace, but now she'd started re-arranging his room and tut-tutting over the state of his wardrobe.

Right that was it. If he couldn't beat them...

'I'm going out on my bike.'

'Aren't you going to finish this game?' Dad said, moving into Paul's vacated chair.

Paul took a crumpled sweatshirt off his bed and searched under his bed for the cycle pump. Glancing back as he left his bedroom, he shook his head in disbelief at the hypocrisy of parents. Dad was glued to the screen, zapping alien space ships while Mum wittered about football. He'd probably return to find her lobbing a football through the azalea bushes. What a crackpot family!

'An outcast even from my own bedroom,' Paul muttered aloud as he trundled his bike out of the garage and set off. The wind was quite sharp in his ears but he rattled off up Roselake Hill and soon warmed up. He cycled aimlessly for about five miles, right up to the recreation ground where he watched some little kids kicking a ball about for a while, then down to the canal and back into his estate. It was still early and he felt like some half-sane company so he continued past the end of his road and carried on to Anthony's house. He'd never been there before but Anthony had said to call half a dozen times. Now was as good a time as any.

Mrs Ahmed answered the door. She had a very round, chubby face and apprehensive expression as if she was afraid of visitors. Paul explained who he was and her face changed.

'Oh, come on in. How nice of you to call. You must be hungry after all that cycling. Now what will it be? Cake, biscuits or some warm naan bread. We love Indian food. I made some for tea.'

Paul decided he was obliged, purely out of polite-
ness, to accept Mrs Ahmed's hospitality and said yes to
everything offered. Anthony came downstairs and
seemed glad to see him.

'Do you want to see my new computer game? Got
it last weekend.'

'Great, yeah.'

'You two go up – I'll bring some drinks up later.'

Paul was impressed. Anthony's bedroom was twice
the size of his, with a huge area for his computer and
stereo. He had his own TV, a video recorder and twice
the number of games he owned. Anthony saw him
eyeing the disks and promptly offered to lend any he
liked the look of. Paul wished he'd visited sooner.
They could do some useful swaps. It was also more
fun competing against someone rather than just
playing a machine. Two hours sped by before Paul
knew it. He'd consumed three wedges of saffron cake
and two chunks of naan bread before Mrs Ahmed
tapped on the door to suggest that he phoned home
or let her husband give him a lift.

'It's all right, Mrs Ahmed,' said Paul. 'I've got lights
on my bike and it's only a little way down the hill.
Thanks for having me.'

'We're very pleased to welcome any of Anthony's
friends.' She was very formal and correct but Paul
liked her. She'd get on well with his mum. Somehow
he had a feeling that the Ahmeds as a family could do
with some friends.

'See you tomorrow. Come round my place for tea
after school.'

Anthony looked pleased but a bit offish at the same
time.

'I thought that was your football night.'

'Tuesdays? Oh no, I go to church youth club,' Paul lied. 'Why not come along with me? Anyone can go.' Paul wished he hadn't added that. It came out sounding like, 'they accept anyone at that place', rather than, 'you don't have to be a member' – which was what he'd meant.

Mrs Ahmed looked so pleased though that he decided he was just getting paranoid on their behalf.

'Anthony would love to, wouldn't you, Anthony?'

Paul glanced at the boy pityingly. He'd be thinking, why can't she let me talk for myself?

'Let me know tomorrow at school,' he added casually, in case Anthony wanted a get-out clause. Paul knew only too well what it felt like being forced into things.

He thought Anthony might make an excuse at school the next day but instead he talked about it several times and seemed quite keen. As the day wore on Paul found himself quite looking forward to it as well, despite the eight week gap since he'd last been.

Mum made toad-in-the-hole for tea and when Anthony kept saying it was the best Yorkshire batter he'd ever tasted, Paul felt a little less embarrassed about the odds and ends of cutlery and plates which they used for weekdays. After Anthony's house, his suddenly seemed really small and shabby. Anthony however didn't even seem to notice and chatted away to his mum as if he'd known her all his life. Paul began to realise that life might be a lot easier if he didn't care quite so much about what other people thought or said. He despised himself for caring so much, especially since most of the time it was about people he didn't even like. Daft really – he just couldn't seem to help himself.

Just before they left for youth club, Grandma came round. Paul's dad had collected her so that Mum could wash and set her hair for some anniversary party she was going to. Gran was in her eighties but a sharp old bird with thick white hair and crooked teeth. Paul was taller than her these days – he couldn't tell whether he had grown or she had shrunk. At any rate, she could make her opinions known pretty forcefully. She demonstrated that as soon as she got in the front room and settled her heavy twill skirt around her knees.

'You want to get Brian out there cleaning the windows. They're filthy!'

'He's been a bit busy, Mum.'

'Neighbours always judge you by your windows.'

'Well, I don't think...'

'Don't want to throw good money at window cleaners, though.'

'You do, Gran,' Paul interrupted, grinning.

'That's different, lad. When I was your mother's age I was washing windows every week. We used to take a pride in it then.'

'Not like today's housewives, eh Gran?' Paul said, egging her on.

His mum took a mock swipe at him with Gran's hairbrush.

At that moment Anthony came in from the hall. The old lady's face was a picture. Her craggy jaw nearly hit her massive bosom. Paul and his mum both tried to distract her at the same time and spoke over each other. In the space, Anthony came forward.

'Hello,' he said and extended a hand towards the old lady. When she didn't move or speak Paul blurted out, 'She's deaf,' just as his mum said, 'She's a bit blind.'

31

'I am not!' The old lady shook herself and, assuming Anthony's hand was there to haul her out of the chair, swung herself up, nearly pulling him onto her lap.

'Now then, let's get a good look at you.'

'This is Anthony, Gran, he's just started at my school.'

'Over here on holiday are you, lad?'

Anthony looked puzzled. 'We've moved here from Birmingham.'

'Birmingham! Ah yes, there's a lot of you over there, aren't there? Bill and I went there once – more black faces than white. Funny thing that, in your own country.'

Paul was aghast. Even his mother was unexpectedly dumb-struck. Anthony's face was expressionless. He just assumed a far-off kind of look. Paul supposed it was his way of dealing with it. Too late, Gran was hauled off to have her hair washed, leaving Paul in a state of confusion. He couldn't apologise for the silly old bird without further embarrassing his guest so he pretended nothing had happened and then couldn't decide whether that made it look as if he agreed with the silly old bat. He hoped rather fervently that his mum drowned the old trout. As fast as he could, Paul bundled Anthony out of the house, talking about all kinds of rubbish so as to avoid any awkward silences.

Thankfully St Lawrence's wasn't far away and music was blaring out of the windows of the adjoining community centre where the youth club met. Simon, the curate, met them at the door and didn't make any comments about the number of weeks Paul had missed. He acted as if they were both regulars. Paul bought a couple of cans of coke and put their names down for the pool competition. He and Anthony were rubbish but so were most of the others and they ended up half way up the league for the week.

There were a couple of decent-looking girls who Paul decided must be new, or maybe they'd just bought contact lenses and a more efficient acne cream. One of them kept glancing at Anthony. Paul wondered whether Anthony was good-looking. At any rate he didn't seem to put females off like Alan always had. Alan was just plain mouthy. He'd have a lot in common with Paul's gran. The memory of that still rankled. And she was supposed to be a Christian. She'd be in church on Sunday, singing hymns about loving all the people of the world – all the people who were white and lived in Stoneysteadman more like.

'Nice to see your friend, Paul,' Simon the curate said. 'He seems to have settled in really well.'

'Yeah, it's been okay here,' Paul agreed, surprised to find just how easy it had been. He hadn't heard one stupid racist joke all night and several of the other kids had spoken to Anthony of their own accord. He was playing darts with a couple of them right now. Paul recalled with shame how, at football practice with Alan, he'd made fun of the youth club with its no-smoking, no swearing, no anything-you-could-think-of rules. At least there was no bullying, no humiliating and no keeping up with everyone. You could be a bit more yourself here without an eye to your street cred all the time.

'We need someone to help organise the junior football team, Saturday mornings. I wondered if you and your friend would be interested?'

'Anthony's not much into football.'

'Well, you on your own then. I know how good you are.'

'I'm not sure,' Paul said evasively. Playing was one thing, organising a rabble of little kids was something else.

'Aw, go on Paul,' said a little dark-haired boy who Paul had seen at the park the previous evening. He had no idea how the kid knew him. 'Me mate says you're dead good – go on, be our coach.'

'Well, I'll see. I might manage it, I suppose, just for a couple of weeks.'

'Great, Paul's gonna be our new coach!' the kids chorused.

'Can't back out now!' Simon warned.

Paul shrugged as if it was a real bind but secretly felt pleased that his skill had been noticed, if only by a couple of pint-pots.

By the end of the evening Paul felt more cheerful than he had done for days. The shadow of school had receded, along with Alan's taunts and hostility. At least he and Anthony were accepted here. They'd had a laugh, nobody had been obnoxious or embarrassing and he hadn't spent the evening looking over his shoulder for trouble. They parted at Stoneman's Stores and Paul jogged home feeling quite pleased with life.

He felt less pleased when he noticed Dad's car still on the drive which meant Gran hadn't gone home yet. Thank goodness he was on his own. It came to something when you had to protect friends from your own family. Gran was holding court about something or other when he slipped into the kitchen and as usual, Mum was just sitting there letting her criticise. He felt really annoyed that his mother never said, 'Shut up, you silly bat!' although she must have been itching to do so for years.

'You don't want to use that margarine rubbish in your cakes, Sheila. Butter, that's the thing. And English, too.'

'We always use Danish, don't we, Mum?' Paul questioned innocently as he rummaged in the fridge. He felt like stirring his gran up tonight. Mum shot him a warning look which he pretended not to understand.

'Should always support the British economy. I always have done,' Gran continued, giving everyone the kind of look which defied all argument.

'Well our house would be really empty if we did that,' Paul whistled.

'Yes, well, who'd like tea?' Mum said.

'That's not English either,' Paul murmured. Gran glared at him, aware that she was being wound up. She decided to change her tack.

'Where's the darkie then?'

'His name's Anthony, Gran,' Paul said pronouncing his name very slowly and clearly as if Gran really was a bit deaf or senile, or both.

'Moved in on the estate have they? Big family, I expect – all that lot do.'

'He's an only child, Gran,' Paul contained his exasperation with difficulty.

'What do they want with a big house then? Didn't you say they were the four-bedroomed houses, Sheila?'

'I expect they can afford it, Mum. Anthony's dad's a computer programmer at Rexels. Quite high up.'

'Yes, taking white folks' jobs. It didn't ought to be allowed.'

35

'Now, Mum, that Dr Cararachi you had at the hospital in Bristol was wonderful, you said so yourself,' Dad reminded her.

'Oh well, that's true, I suppose. Live and let live I say. There's good and bad everywhere. Seemed a nice enough lad, that Anthony,' she added as an afterthought.

Paul was astonished. She'd just talked herself round in a complete circle and tomorrow no doubt she would trot out all the same illogical prejudices to whoever would listen.

'Drink up, Mum, let's get you home.' Dad smiled good humouredly.

Mum kissed her affectionately, packed her off with a tin of the fairy cakes, and stood in the freezing cold drive until the car had disappeared from view.

Paul was watching TV when his mum returned and collapsed on the sofa. She looked exhausted.

'How do you put up with her?' Paul demanded.

He hadn't meant to start on his mum but he just didn't understand how anyone could listen to that for a whole evening without perpetrating some dreadful crime.

''What do you mean, love?' Mum gazed at him in genuine surprise.

'Gran! She's always on at you.'

'Oh that!' Mum laughed. 'It's just old folks set in their ways. Change can be a bit frightening, you know, especially if you feel you're losing your grip.'

'Gran certainly isn't. She has a stranglehold on you and Dad. One squawk and you're running at her beck and call.'

'Hardly. Anyway, she's family,' Mum said, as if that answered it all.

'I could have died when she started on Anthony.'

'Oh yes, I know. I was sorry about that. I hope you explained to Anthony.'

'Explained what, Mum? That my gran is a bigoted old crone with no manners?'

'Paul!'

'Well it's true.'

'Now you listen here, young man. Before you go criticising people, just you think about where they come from, and what they've been brought up with.'

Paul stared at the television screen blankly with a rebellious frown. Mum rested a hand on his tense shoulder and squeezed it gently.

'Look, Paul, most of our opinions come from our parents, our homes and what we see around us. Gran never saw a black person, except in books and on the television, until she was in her sixties. You know what it's like around here. You're not a local until you've lived here for thirty years or been born here; outsiders never mix easily. She thought Anthony was polite – that's a start. Your dad will have a word about it with her, but in her generation calling someone a darkie or whatever isn't being offensive. It's just a word she grew up with.'

'Well what about all that rubbish about supporting the English?'

'Old-fashioned patriotism. Kids were taught it at school. She believes in it. You can't shift that overnight – maybe never.'

'So Gran can say whatever she likes?' Paul retorted.

'She has a right to be listened to. We don't have to agree with her. We can make up our own minds and I hope you always will.'

'But she goes to church, Mum, spouting all that...'

Paul was going to say 'rubbish' but out of deference to his mum he changed to... 'all those odd opinions, and they're not Christian at all.'

'Church isn't just for saints − far from it. It's for people − all people, the good, the bad and the ugly! Christians aren't perfect either. They believe they have a need of God and that the way to know him is through Jesus. They believe God can change them and help them to deal with their problems. Then they try to help other people too.'

'I never know what to say to people to help them,' Paul confessed.

'You're like your father. You both think a lot. Me, I just come straight out with things, not always the right things.'

'I wish I didn't do so much thinking sometimes,' Paul admitted. 'It gets in the way.'

'I hope you'll be grateful that you can think before you act. So many people can't.'

'Like Alan.'

'Really?' Paul's mum waited.

'He did something really stupid when Anthony joined the school.'

'Is that why you've fallen out?'

'Yes, but not just about that. It's sort of grown, and I can't stop it.'

'Have you given him a chance to make up with you?'

'Don't be daft, Mum. He hates my guts.'

'I doubt it.'

'Well, I hate his.' Paul scowled at the carpet and picked at stray threads viciously.

'So it's stalemate. And you're just as entrenched as your grandmother who you've been criticising so freely tonight!'

'It's not the same,' Paul deluded himself.

Paul's mum tucked her feet under her and ran a hand through her soft brown hair. It reached just below her jawline and was sort of girlish. Paul liked it, just as he had done as a small child, when he'd wound it round his fingers when he was being carried in her arms.

'Sometimes,' she said, closing her eyes thoughtfully, 'people are nasty because we don't give them a chance to back down or say sorry. We trap them just as much as they trap themselves.'

'Alan wouldn't be sorry in a million years. It's not like him. If he can't have people who agree blindly with him, he's just not interested.'

'In that case I can't imagine why you are the least bit worried about not being friends with him any more.'

'It was just over Anthony, at least it was at first, then, well, he's got a personal grudge against me.'

'Perhaps he wishes he hadn't been so hasty. You've got to remember that, like Gran, the Ackfords have been a part of this community for donkey's years. The Ackfords have never lived above twenty miles from where they do now. Alan will have listened to his gran and grandpa, his father and all those brothers of his – they're as stuck in the mud and racist as any family I know.'

'So Alan isn't responsible for his own actions?' Paul was dubious. It sounded like a cop-out to him.

'I'm not saying that exactly, but it's easy to see why he's as racist as he is. If you turn your back on him, as the only friend he's ever had who isn't going to go along with everything he does all the time, then he hasn't a chance of changing or seeing that there's

39

another way of looking at things.'

'He doesn't care what I think,' Paul argued. 'He doesn't need me.'

'If he wasn't the slightest bit concerned, he wouldn't have kept up this war against you. My guess is he feels rejected by you – he may even be jealous of Anthony for taking you away. Alan is one of life's natural bullies because he can't trust people unless he's the boss. That's why he surrounds himself with wimps.'

'I was one of them,' Paul laughed.

'But not any more. Your dad and I are really proud of you for not giving in to peer pressure. That's all it is – but it's pretty powerful. Too many kids get caught up in it. They never think for a moment about what they're doing or why. They just follow the crowd. If more people were independent and did what they wanted to, this would be a much healthier society. And never think the church is for wets. It takes courage to say you believe in something that the crowd doesn't. We're supposed to be so free and easy these days – you know, anything goes, but somehow it just isn't like that. Every generation has its problems. You'll be no different from your gran, I'm afraid.'

Paul groaned. 'Don't say that!'

'You wait and see, my lad!'

3

After several more evenings spent either at Anthony's house or up in his own room playing on the computer, Paul's mum finally put her foot down. 'You're addicted to these wretched games,' she announced, coming into his bedroom.

'Hm,' Paul murmured, eyes glued to the screen and oblivious to her ranting.

'Right, that's it!' With one bound she was across the room and flicked off the main switch.

'Mum!' Paul shouted. 'You're supposed to stop the program.'

'I just did.'

'Not like that. I was on level 14, now it's not saved and I'm back on level 1. It's taken me all week to get to where I was.'

'It's a game, Paul, and you play it far too much. Enough's enough. The computer stays off for the next week.'

'What?' Paul couldn't believe it.

'Half-term begins at the weekend. You can get out and do something in the fresh air. I don't mind what, but I don't want you stuck in front of that screen for another minute.'

Paul opened his mouth to protest but closed it when he saw the expression on his mother's face. It would be pointless to argue. 'And what *am* I supposed to do, then?'

'Go out with your friends.'

'What friends?' he glowered.

'If you can't find anything to do, your dad's got plenty of jobs for you. Start with the garage. You can get that swept and tidied, then the hedge needs trimming. I don't think you'll be bored,' she smiled sweetly and swept out of the room.

Right, Paul thought, I'll sit here and do nothing. Presumably that'll make her happy. Five minutes later Paul could stand it no longer. In a foul temper, he stomped downstairs, slammed the front door and headed for the garage.

What a mess! He shook a cement bag which sent spirals of dust into the air and started picking up the odd bits of oily cloth, broken shards of metal and off-cuts of wood scattered over the floor. He wound the 80 feet of hose pipe, which was coiled like a slack snake, into a reasonable bundle and stuffed it into a plastic barrel.

Paul was disconcerted to find that a lot of the rubbish belonged to him. Old footballs, cricket bats, fishing nets and the remains of various model-making experiments littered the work bench and tools were all over the place. It was a tedious job and as his jeans became more encrusted with grime and the dust choked him, so his mood worsened.

Anthony's arrival was a welcome relief. He sat on an upturned tea chest and surveyed the operation with critical eyes.

'Are you coming over to play computers?'

'No, I'm cutting the hedge,' Paul grumbled.

'Oh well, if you'd rather cut the hedge.'

'Of course I wouldn't rather cut the hedge. I'm banned from computers.'

'Come round to my place, then your mum won't know what you're doing.'

Paul shook the damp tendrils of smooth blond hair out of his eyes and wrinkled his freckled nose. 'Can't,' he said simply.

'Why not?' Anthony was puzzled.

Paul shrugged. He felt hard done by, infuriated by his mother and generally fed up but it didn't occur to him to go behind her back. She'd know, she always did. But that wasn't all. He just wouldn't go off and do what she'd explicitly told him not to.

Anthony wiped his nose and sneezed. 'You're making too much dust.'

'Tell me something I don't know.'

'You want to damp it down.'

Paul looked up and thought about various abusive comments he could make.

'Here, I'll show you.' Anthony grabbed the battered watering-can and went off to fill it. 'It would be better with a sprinkler but this'll have to do.'

He started dousing the dirty floor with water, slopping it into the farthest corner. Finally he stood in the middle of the garage and spun round, watering-can outstretched, doing a 'Singing in the Rain' impersonation. Paul scowled at the mess but had to admit it did make the sweeping up easier.

'There you are. Get some brains behind the operation.'

'A bit more brawn wouldn't go amiss,' Paul pouted.

'Can't be done, my son. You're banned from computers, I'm on a death threat if I get these jeans dirty – not on the first day anyway. You've missed a bit over there.'

Paul raised the broom and waved its soggy head in the direction of Anthony's knees.

He had to admit that Anthony's company was better than being alone. Even cleaning the garage didn't seem as daunting. He sat down beside Anthony and surveyed his handiwork – not brilliant but a definite improvement. The five sacks of rubbish were Dad's problem to dispose of. 'Just the hedge to go, love,' Mum said, appearing round the corner with two glasses of coke.

'Oh Mum – give us a break!'

'No problem, we'll have that done in no time,' Anthony said, his brown eyes sparkling.

'Be careful with the clippers. I don't want anyone electrocuted,' Mum warned, as Paul brandished the tool light-heartedly over the sagging box hedge which separated their house from the neighbours.

'Here, I've got an idea,' Anthony said, relieving him of the clippers.

'I thought you couldn't get dirty?'

'This is clean work. Watch this, I saw a programme on topiary the other day.'

'Top what?'

'Cutting hedges into shapes of animals and things. What do you fancy? A cow, a dog?'

'I don't think Mum...'

Too late. Anthony was already slicing great wedges

out of the hedge, waving the clippers about like a paintbrush. Paul went to fetch a rake but in the tidied garage spent ten minutes hauling it out of the old wardrobe, where he'd stacked it behind all the other implements. When he returned, the sight of the hedge made him feel momentarily weak.

'What is it?' he yelled.

Anthony gave him a reproachful look. 'Can't you tell?'

'Funnily enough no. It looks like someone's lobbed a grenade in the middle of it. What on earth is my mother going to say?'

'It's a cockerel.'

'Where?' Paul was amazed that Anthony could actually claim that the twisted twigs sticking up from a hump in the middle of the hedge represented anything at all.

'Look, there's its beak and there's that bit under its throat.'

'Oh yes, I see it now. And its five legs.'

'You just don't appreciate the skill of topiary.'

'I might if I saw some!'

'I'll just tidy it up a bit.'

'Oh no, you don't. That's enough, thank you very much.' Paul relieved him of the clippers and made a valiant if unsuccessful attempt to redeem what was left of the hedge. He decided, after removing the cockerel's head and tail (he still couldn't say which end was which) that he'd better just clear up very conscientiously and leave it at that. His mother was going to go mad. They swept like fury, dumped all the bits on the compost and set off on their bikes. She might as well have a couple of hours to calm down before he faced her.

45

'That was fun. Dad never lets me do anything around the house, says it's too dangerous,' Anthony mused as they pedalled up the lane.

'You can understand that, and I don't think it's your safety he's worried about either.'

'What shall we do then?'

'We can go up on the common. The Army were training last week – might be some shells to collect.'

'All right then – race you!'

Anthony set off, legs going like pistons, his initial surge putting him a couple of lengths ahead of Paul. They fought for the lead up the hill, until Paul's front wheel hit a pot-hole and sent him tumbling down the grassy verge, grazing elbows and chin.

'Beat you!' Anthony grinned, holding a hand out to haul Paul up.

The army road went higher and was so badly deteriorated in parts that they stashed their bikes and continued on foot.

Scouting around the firing range and inside the bunkers, the boys managed to find several rounds of spent ammunition, bits of shell and shrapnel. The sun was hot on their backs and Paul could feel the skin on his arms tingling. Anthony's glossy dark skin was coarser textured than his own and the sweat formed raised droplets.

'I bet you never get sunburnt, do you?' Paul observed.

Anthony grinned. 'Look at this.' He flipped his watch strap off proudly to display his tan. 'That's just from last week. I don't go lobster like you though.'

'Lucky you. This'll be itching like mad tonight. I just get covered in freckles. Mum's bought me some factor 30 something. I used it last year and didn't put

46

it on all over – ended up looking scabby with some completely white patches.'

They sat and panted, backs against a rock. 'Do you have to comb your hair?'

'Na, I don't bother. I have it cut a lot.'

'Does it grow then?'

'Course it does – a heck of a lot. Touch it – go on.'

Paul put out a tentative finger. It was really springy and tough. 'Hey, that's pretty cool!' he said, bouncing the flat of his palm up and down on Anthony's head. 'It'd make a great trampoline for hamsters.'

'I'll bear that in mind. Hey, there's not much to do around here, is there?'

Paul sighed. He quite liked it in the country but he supposed it must be a bit dull after Birmingham.

'Nothing ever happens here, does it?'

Paul opened his mouth to protest but shut it again. Their local newspaper must be the biggest disappointment an ambitious young journalist could imagine. There had been a nasty attack of vandalism on the rose bushes outside the men's loos in town – that had kept the police busy for a while but, generally speaking, charity cycle rides and protests over the proposed bypass made up the bulk of the local news. Not exactly Dodge City.

'Dad gave me a fiver,' Anthony said, getting up. 'Let's cycle into town and get a burger.'

'All right.'

They jogged back down to their bikes and rode into town. In Burger King, they sat at the nailed-down plastic chairs and bit into double cheese burgers with pleasure. They shared a thick chocolate shake that was so glutinous it hardly went up the straw.

'When I'm older,' Anthony said, 'I'll live on burgers

and chips and never look at a fresh vegetable again.'

'You get the lettuce in here,' Paul said, with his mouth full.

'Exactly – perfectly balanced meal.'

Full up, they wandered through town, looking in shop windows. Paul realised that, for the past fortnight – since falling out with Alan in fact, he hadn't worried about new clothes or the latest bag with the right label. Anthony had some good gear, no doubt about that, but he didn't go on about it – never picked holes in everybody else's stuff. He hadn't made a single comment about Paul's house or his dad's old Vauxhall. If Alan had lived where Anthony did and had all that expensive gear in his bedroom, he'd have been ramming it down everyone's throat.

It came to Paul, yet again, that Anthony was a much easier person to be with. So if that was the case, why did he still feel so lost without Alan and the gang? He wished he didn't care so much about street cred and fitting in. In some ways it was easier to be like Anthony – at least being completely different gave you some kind of status. For over a week now nobody had said or done anything to Anthony at school. It was almost as if they were afraid of him. For a start, all the teachers were on his side, and constantly checking he was okay. They'd never be that bothered about most kids. Paul still remembered his first term with a shudder. He'd suffered a thousand agonies being left on his own during Science practicals or drama. It was pretty tough having a brainstorming session with yourself. But then Anthony had *him*. It made Paul feel kind of noble and warm inside. Maybe Alan had felt that way when he'd first taken Paul into his gang. Funny thing, friendships.

They unchained their cycles and meandered down to the canal. A couple of men were fishing, otherwise the tow-path was deserted. They sat with their feet in the water for a while. The sun beat down on their backs, unexpectedly hot for the time of year.

'Let's swim,' Anthony said, jumping up.

'We've got no towels or swimming shorts.'

'I thought you country people just stripped off at the first hint of summer! Come on.'

Reluctantly, Paul stripped to his underwear and dabbled one foot in the water. It was freezing. 'Geronimo!' Anthony yelled and launched himself into the canal with a belly-slapping crash. One of the fishermen shook his head in disbelief and started to pack up.

'I think you've frightened the fish away,' Paul said, as he gritted his teeth and slid in.

'What a stupid idea,' he moaned, making little doggy-paddle strokes while Anthony bobbed up and down like a drunken cork.

'You wimp! Get those legs working.'

'Leave off! You're splashing me!'

'What an old woman.'

'You won't say that when you swallow the blue-green algae, or get dragged under by the bed-springs.'

Anthony looked down at the weeds waving between his knees. 'Come on – over to the other side.'

'You swim like you play football!' Paul called. They hauled themselves out on the far side and dried off in the sun. A light wind had whipped up and it was freezing against Paul's damp skin which was all goose-flesh. They lay on their backs silently for a while until a sudden angry hissing made both boys shoot up. An enormous male swan, neck outstretched and powerful beak parted, was advancing on them. Up close the bird was frightening.

'He must have a nest nearby,' Paul warned. 'Come on – those things can break your arm.'

'What – with their beaks?' Anthony's appalled look was hilarious.

'No, you fool, with their wings. I'm not hanging round to give you a demonstration, anyway.'

Surprising himself with his athleticism, Paul dived back into the water, slicing through half the width of the canal. From the commotion behind, it sounded as if the swan was close on their tails.

'Vicious blinking thing,' Anthony cried, as he jumped up on the tow-path.

'Mind your clothes – you're soaking them.'

'Never mind that – the thing nearly had me.'

From the safety of the bank, both boys calmed down a bit. 'Fantastic creatures,' Paul sighed, as they watched the big bird circle intimidatingly.

'What sort of nest does it have?'

'Don't you know that?' Paul said.

'There weren't a lot of swans in the middle of Birmingham,' Anthony returned sarcastically.

'I suppose not. Well, their nests are sort of raft things – dead scruffy. Just a load of sticks and reeds piled together – not a nest at all really.'

'Where do they build them?'

'Anywhere they like, with a beak like that,' Paul commented dryly.

'I'd like to see it sometime.'

'They don't like to be disturbed. She's either on the eggs or they've only just hatched – that's why he's so protective. They mate for life, you know.'

'Hm. I suppose there are *some* interesting things

round here,' Anthony smiled.

They dressed, still damp. Anthony's hair shed water in a trice while Paul's wet tendrils dripped water down his back, soaking his T-shirt.

'Here, do you want one?' Anthony held out a pack of cigarettes which he'd retrieved from his pocket.

Paul wrinkled his nose, 'No thanks.'

Anthony didn't push it, but he took a long drag from the lit cigarette and blew it between his teeth with practised ease.

'Do your parents mind you smoking?' Paul asked.

'They don't know.'

'I bet they can smell it on you!'

'I always keep some mints in my pocket.'

'How do you get the cigarettes? Taylors won't sell to under sixteens.'

'They're the only ones who won't then! You can get them from the kiosk in town. Actually I've got a few packets from friends in Birmingham – kind of leaving present. Have one if you want.'

'I tried it once.' Paul had vivid memories of his first smoke with Alan. He'd nearly thrown up. He'd been so white when he got home that Mum had insisted on dosing him up with liver salts and then he really *had* thrown up.

'Everyone's sick first time. You have to keep at it.'

'Why?'

'I like it now.'

'Oh.' Paul had always been glad that he'd had the excuse of football as a fair reason not to smoke. Alan had made him feel a bit of a wimp at first but even he had cut down a bit after the Science lessons where they'd seen videos of diseased lungs cut open. It always amazed Paul that people could watch that and then go straight out at break and smoke a fag. The Science teacher was one of the worst. His prep room was like a *Benson and Hedges* trial lab. Yet he was the first inside the fume cupboard when they started sulphur experiments.

Anthony pulled on his cigarette and lay back in the sun.

Paul smiled at the memory of Alan purchasing his first box of condoms from a vending machine. Without a chance in the world of ever needing them, he'd carried them around in his pocket for three months last year until Karen had seen them and nearly died laughing and then kept asking if he'd checked the sell-by date. Alan had thrown them away in his bin at home and his mum had found them. She'd been so worried about her son having unprotected sex that she bought him a load more and kept leaving them in obvious places. He could have had quite a trade going with the sixth formers but he was so embarrassed about it, especially when she left one in his lunch box one day. He confessed to his mum that he'd never used one and, thanks to her, probably never ever would.

Anthony sat up and blinked. 'What now then? Are there any arcades in town?'

'There's the Silver Gun down Fore Street.'

'Come on then. I've got a quid left and I'm feeling lucky.'

'It's a waste of money,' Paul said, resolutely refusing to be drawn into the game as Anthony flicked and stabbed at buttons. Almost before the words were out of his mouth, Anthony hit the Jackpot and a shower of tokens tumbled down the chute.

'Can't leave now,' Anthony smiled.

'You could cash them in.'

'We're not old enough – he'll tell us to clear off. Come on – half each, but this time we'll play for cash. Over here. Put those computer skills of yours to good use. Perhaps your mum'll change her mind then.'

Paul raised his eyes and hoped no one recognised him in here. His parents certainly wouldn't approve. Trouble was, it *was* alluring – all the flashing lights and noise. He watched a couple of older men playing the machines. Their faces were absolutely intent, their eyes mesmerised by the rolling symbols. Paul lost his pound almost immediately and fed in two more which went the same way. He won a couple of games and recouped some of his losses but then piled it straight back in. Madness really. How did people get like that? It was kind of spooky.

Paul looked at the tokens in his hand and then pushed them into the first machine he came to. He wanted to be out of here and Anthony with him. In spite of his casual approach he won a couple of times but then, true to form, the machine swallowed the lot and Paul turned away, glad. The catchy tune didn't attract him. All he could see was the face of the old man pressed haggardly to the fruit machine in the corner. He shuddered and went to find Anthony who was still playing a game.

'Come on, we shouldn't be in here. Let's go.'

'Hang on, I'm winning.'

'Well, if you're not coming with me, I'm going alone.'

Anthony frowned, his eyes flickered from the screen to Paul and back again. Paul moved away, determined now not to stay another second.

'Wait up, I'm on the last… oh all right.' Anthony

slapped the machine and followed Paul out. They blinked in the sunshine and wandered slowly back to the recreation ground where they had locked their bikes. It was about half past four and time to be heading home. Paul had to face his mum – the memory of the hedge flooded back in full force. He decided not to invite Anthony back. His mum in one of her rare rages wasn't a pretty sight. It would be better to start for home after his dad had got back. He would be on the receiving end of the worst of his wife's anger and then he'd have her laughing about it, with any luck.

'Hey, what are those kids up to?' Anthony cried, nudging Paul in the ribs as he broke into a trot.

The group of lads about their age were larking about on the towpath. One of them had a rifle and was pinging old tin cans about. The cans jumped and spiralled about as the lead shots hit them. Unfortunately, the fishermen had gone and the place was deserted. Kids and their mothers from the adjoining recreation ground had gone home for their tea long ago.

'Let's just get our bikes and go,' Paul urged. 'We don't want any trouble.' He didn't like to sound cowardly but in view of the fact that they were only two, while there were about five of the other lads, discretion definitely seemed favourable.

'They shouldn't be shooting that thing out here,' Anthony said. 'Anyone could get hit.'

'Yeah, and it could be us, so let's go. If you feel so public-spirited we'll report them to the police on the way home.' Paul got onto his bike and pushed off. He recognised a couple of the lads and knew their reputations for unprovoked arguments. They'd left school last year but still hung around outside the gates waiting for mates who were in the sixth form. The other boys were much younger and Paul didn't know them, but he wasn't over-keen to get acquainted. Quite apart from anything else, they were the types who would pick on them just because of Anthony's colour and Paul didn't want to expose his friend to that.

Anthony was hesitating but had turned his cycle homeward when they heard a crash in the canal followed by the now familiar hissing sound. Someone screamed, there was laughter and then two shots were fired.

'They're going after the swan!' Anthony cried, throwing his cycle to the ground. Paul looked over his shoulder in horror as Anthony sped off after the group, shouting loudly and waving his arms.

'That kid's going to get his head kicked in,' Paul muttered as he dropped his bike and followed. For someone devoted to keeping out of trouble, he was anticipating yet another tricky situation. It was getting to be too dangerous being around Anthony. Around the next bend he almost ran straight into two of the younger lads. They were legging it down the path, pursued by the male swan. Ahead, Anthony was making a spirited attack on the older lad with the gun. Anthony would have been in trouble but a second swan, presumably the female, was lunging at the boy's leg so he couldn't concentrate on Anthony. His friend had grabbed a branch and was hurling it about near their heads, though it wasn't clear which of the two he was more likely to hit.

Paul launched himself at the boy with such ferocity that they both ended up on the ground with a mouthful of grit. Fortunately the branch fell out of the other's grasp and he was too winded by Paul's knee in his stomach to retaliate. Paul sat up and spat grass out. The lad under him looked at him with puzzled, dazed eyes. Paul felt an absurd desire to say sorry but he restrained himself. Instead he stuck his knee in just hard enough to bring tears to the eyes of his adversary before rolling off him.

Ah! Paul spun round in alarm to see the swan launch a fresh attack on the boy with the gun. Spurred on by fear of those flapping wings in his face, he wrenched away from Anthony's grip and hobbled away after the youngsters. His crony joined him, clutching his stomach in pain.

When they were out of range of the swan, the one with the gun yelled back some obscenity and a threat, but they weren't up to pressing the point at that moment.

Paul dusted himself down and turned to Anthony who was kneeling on the edge of the canal.

'Are you all right?' Paul said, suddenly alarmed.

'Yes, I'm fine but look.'

Paul squinted over his friend's shoulder, keeping a respectful eye on the swan who was still making a demented racket further up the canal. Floating in the canal were the remains of three eggs, large white ovals smashed open by gunshot. The disturbed nest was just beneath them on a kind of natural jetty. If they'd looked a bit closer that afternoon they'd easily have spotted it.

'The filthy swine!' Anthony's eyes were bloodshot and nearly bolting from his head with rage. His hands made impotent fists. 'I'd like to smash their faces in.'

'Come away, be quiet,' Paul urged. 'Look, there are

four more. She may go back to them.'

'She'll desert them – bound to.'

'Not necessarily. Come on, give her a chance to calm down.'

His face creased with anguish, Anthony stumbled back from the edge and allowed himself to be led back onto the tow-path. Behind a clump of teasels they crouched down and watched as the two swans were reunited upstream and circled nervously. It was an eternity before they approached the nest site but at last they disappeared in the undergrowth and Paul felt reasonably confident that the female had decided to settle herself back on the eggs.

It was only then, as they turned away, that the shock and cold hit him. He couldn't believe he'd actually ended up in a fight and could still walk.

'I'm not going to let them do that again,' Anthony said, as he picked his bike up. 'We're going to look after them,' he said, staring into Paul's eyes.

Paul shivered, 'I know.'

Over half-term, Anthony and Paul spent nearly every daylight hour down at the canal. Paul's parents had phoned the Council and some wire and notices had been put up around the nest site. An RSPB representative had visited and the game warden from the common agreed to include the nest on his daily duties to try to dissuade the youths from returning. There was even an article in the newspaper with an editorial about how important it was to protect the local swans who had only just returned to the canal after years of pollution had driven them away.

The boys remained doubtful about such publicity. They knew a few people who would go down and have a look just because it was out of bounds, and others with more sinister intentions who would get ideas from the story.

The swans were no more friendly to the boys than they had been to the louts, but Paul and Anthony continued to guard the site and bring scraps of bread to help the swans in their search for food. They knew food was plentiful really, but the male in particular had a taste for stale saffron cake and perhaps it made up for the barbaric treatment he had experienced from the other humans.

The police had taken a statement from Paul about the gun and the names of the older lads.

Dad thought there wasn't much they could do except issue a warning, but it might have some effect. Being a rural community, a lot of lads had guns. They used them, along with nets, ferrets and dogs, to go rabbiting on the common. Local butchers paid about fifty pence a carcass and it was a good way of making pocket money. Farmers were glad as well. Paul hated hearing about how many rabbits had been caught when boys were chatting at school, but he supposed it was preferable to spreading rabbit diseases, the alternative to such methods of control. The trouble was that certain people with a gun in their hands needed more excitement than just rabbits.

Paul's dad had been quite proud of his son for taking on the louts but Mum had been very quiet and hated him going down to the canal. She even lifted the ban on computer games but to no avail, Paul couldn't waste time on them while the swans needed protection.

'It's only until they hatch,' he explained.

'Well, you'll be back at school on Monday so who looks after them then? All this time down at the canal. I don't like it.'

'Sheila, the lads aren't going to get into any more scuffles. We've talked about that. I think it's pretty public-spirited of them to take this on. A lot of kids would've been bored with it by now. Anyway, love, you know you're always saying they should be out in the fresh air.' Paul's dad winked at him and gestured for him to get going.

Mum, who knew she was being made fun of, didn't respond. She sighed and couldn't quite disguise the worry lines around her mouth despite her smile, but she didn't try to stop Paul. He seemed to have grown up just recently and was so full of determination. She'd always thought he didn't have an ounce of get up and go about him. The new version would take some getting used to.

The boys were inseparable. Even back at school they agreed to cycle down to the canal at lunch time, instead of eating in the canteen, and after school, just to check.

Mr Campbell had seen their pictures in the paper and during the first tutorial made them give a talk on the events. Paul had decided to play down his part – he didn't want anyone to get any ideas that he'd turned into a hard-man overnight. Unfortunately, after Anthony's somewhat exaggerated account of Paul's pinning a six foot giant to the ground and him wrestling the murder weapon from his opponent, their class-mates were agog. Paul groaned inwardly and stole a glance at Alan and the others. He had a contemptuous half-smile on his lips and yawned very loudly to show that he wasn't impressed. Surprisingly Karen told him to shut up and let them listen when he started to heckle and that shut him up more effectively than anything could have done.

Paul would have enjoyed the attention and new hero status except that it put an even greater barrier between him and Alan. Now the comments were frostier and more insulting. He and Anthony were

60

now referred to as 'The Caped Crusader and Robin' only Anthony didn't need the uniform – ha ha.

'Shut up, Alan,' Paul hissed during PE that morning after he'd been called Bird Man twice on the football field.

Alan just laughed and started to hum 'Feed the birds, tuppence a bag.'

Paul was irritated. 'You're pathetic – push off.'

'Tut tut – Sunday School teacher wouldn't like that,' Alan smirked.

It didn't matter what Paul did or said, Alan could get at him. He wished they could make up. He had even tried to talk to him once or twice.

'Look, why don't you come down to the canal with us and see the nest?'

'I've got other birds to watch,' Alan returned. 'You can keep your bird watching with Black Beauty.'

'Oh yeah, started on Year 7 now, have you?' It was out of his mouth before Paul could stop it. A stupid throwaway line in return for all the rubbish he'd had to put up with. Alan's eyes smouldered. He didn't like a taste of his own medicine.

'Year 10 actually,' Alan spat out and stalked off.

The PE teacher caught Paul just as he was leaving. 'Game tonight against Portland High – you're left winger.'

'Oh Sir, I can't tonight.'

'You're in the team, Paul. I've turned other lads down because of you. I think you owe us a bit of loyalty. Don't let all this publicity stuff go to your head, lad.'

Paul was stung by the injustice of all this. He didn't think he owed the team anything, bearing in mind how most of them had treated him recently. And it was unfair about the publicity. He didn't care about that. School was beginning to be a serious pain in the backside. The day didn't go very well. He was in trouble during Science for not writing up a practical which he'd had all half-term to do. It had simply slipped his mind, what with everything else.

'Stay behind tonight, lad,' Reeder ordered.

'Can't Sir, Mr Parr wants me in the football team – away match.'

'We are in demand, aren't we? Lunch time then.'

'But...'

'Vital meeting *then*?' Reeder boomed ominously.

'He's bird-watching!' Alan piped up from the back.

'Get stuffed, Ackford,' Paul shouted back at him.

'Quiet! In here at one o'clock and no excuse,' Reeder yelled, now thoroughly annoyed.

'Yes Sir,' Paul murmured.

'Now then, top marks went to Anthony Ahmed in the test last term. Let's go through that, shall we?'

Paul sighed. The harder he tried to keep everyone happy the more hassle he gave himself. Meanwhile Anthony cruised along without a problem in the world, and if it wasn't for him, things between Paul and Alan would be just as they always had been. Paul spent a miserable lunch time copying up his home-work under the eye of Reeder, who was in a worse mood because he couldn't leave Paul to grab a fag. Why punish himself like this? Paul couldn't figure it out. Anthony went alone to the canal after school, while Paul travelled in the minibus to Portland. Nobody spoke to him and he wondered why on earth Parr had chosen him. Then he discovered Bateman had gone on holiday and he was just a filler.

He didn't play too badly but Alan and Kevin

wouldn't pass properly so he missed several chances. At least he managed a couple of good tackles and at half-time they were one all against a slightly better side. Parr gave them a right rollicking as usual, but he said Paul had done quite well which was pretty good praise from him. Then he tore into Alan and told him he was a selfish player and should pass the ball around more. Paul knew from experience that it wasn't the best psychology to use with Alan who couldn't cope with criticism. For once though, Paul was pleased that Alan had got it in the neck. He was fed up of being the only one in the mire.

They were just getting ready to go back out for the second half when Paul, adjusting his laces, snapped one off at the base. He didn't have a spare pair and the ragged end left wasn't long enough even to knot. He went to Mr Parr who also had no spare. 'Hang on lads, anyone got any spare laces? This is an emergency.'

'Alan has,' someone piped up.

'Good. Ackford, lend Paul your laces, can you? I want to get this half started.'

Alan fetched the laces from his bag with obvious distaste. He almost threw them at Paul and added childishly, 'I want them back at the end of the game.'

Paul remembered all the stuff he'd lent or rather given Alan in the past. How could anyone be that petty? 'Sure,' he said.

The second half was more fluent than the first but the undercurrents on the pitch made it a hostile game. Alan passed to Paul three or four times but never when he was in a space, so inevitably he lost the ball to a defender. Then Alan took the ball right up the field, dribbled past several backs and scored. It was a stupid move really but he'd had his moment of glory.

After that the Portland team got their act together and made Milbain look pretty scrappy for a while, but Kevin in goal kept them in the lead. Paul ran his heart out, determined to give Mr Parr no reason to say he wasn't a team player, but he wasn't that surprised when Portland lobbed in an equaliser ten minutes from the end. Parr ranted and raved from the sideline but the boys were tired. Paul made a reasonable pass to Scott and there was a momentary panic in the box but Portland's goalie saved the fumbled goal and the referee blew the final whistle. Two all. Not a bad result, all things considered, but disappointing after over an hour of pounding up and down.

Paul jogged into the changing-rooms and chucked off his shirt. He couldn't wait to get changed and get home. He'd had enough of being treated like a leper. Alan passed, shoving him in the shoulder on his way to the showers. 'Don't forget the laces,' he snarled.

Paul bent down and pulled his boots off. He ripped the spare lace out and went over to Alan's bag. It was easy to spot with the distinctive logo and stripe. He folded the lace up into a tight little ball and poked his fingers down the side pocket for the plastic bag it had come from. He retrieved the bag and started to stuff the lace in when he realised that it wasn't the right bag. There was something in the bottom, something white... white powder... Paul's hand shook, his brain was doing somersaults.

'What on earth do you think you're doing?'

Paul jumped as if he'd been stung. He leapt up with the bag crumpled into the palm of his hand.

'Alan!' He felt sick and relieved all at the same time.

'What were you doing in my bag?' Alan began self-righteously.

'Oh just cut it out, Alan. I was returning your poxy lace and found this by mistake. I certainly wouldn't go looking for it. Here.' He pushed it roughly in his face and stepped past. Alan grasped his shoulder and swung him round.

'If you breathe a word about this...' he began.

'You'll what?' Paul cut him off. He was sick and tired of being pushed around by Alan and this made him braver than he would normally have been. Alan looked nonplussed. He wasn't used to people standing up to him, especially not Paul. He tried a different tack, anxious to get the upper hand again.

'Look, its none of your business. It's not what you think, anyway.'

'I know just what it is. It's illegal.'

'Yeah well, I'd expect a prissy Sunday School kid to come out with that,' Alan sneered. He had gone red and looked a bit flustered.

Paul remained surprisingly calm. For once the old jibe didn't hurt. He played with Alan. 'If you're not sure that I won't tell perhaps you'd better get your hands off me,' he whispered.

Alan let go immediately. He did a kind of jig around Paul as he moved back to his own peg.

'It's not mine,' he said.

'Try another, Alan.'

'Honest, it's Sharon's, you know, in 10L. We've been going out. She gave me some to try last week. It's nothing. It doesn't even do anything not really – just relaxes you. It's not addictive or anything.'

'Don't try convincing me,' Paul hissed. 'I'm not the jerk carrying it around. And I was there in PSE, too.' Drugs awareness week had been one of the biggest bores of last term.

'It's no big deal then.'

'If you say so,' Paul zipped up his bag deliberately and swung it over his shoulder. He looked Alan squarely in the eye. 'If you're found with that stuff in school you'll be expelled. Being expelled *is* addictive – no other school will touch you.'

Alan went as pale as anyone can go without actually fainting.

'And I'd say your dad'll more or less kill you if that happens.' Paul pushed home his advantage with delicious enjoyment. 'So in a roundabout way, drugs could be very harmful to your health, wouldn't you say?'

Alan murmured something obscene but for once in his life he looked utterly dejected. Momentarily, Paul felt sorry for him. He hadn't realised he was involved with Sharon's group in Year 10. They were into everything. Alan had plenty of friends, so why get mixed up with that crowd?

'I won't say anything, but you've got to flush it down the loo – now.'

Alan's colour filtered back. He shrugged his shoulders with remarkable bravado, and strode over to the cubicles. Paul watched him for a sign of a truce as he returned but there was none. In Alan's ice-blue eyes he could see only hatred and something else, even more dangerous. Was it revenge? He shivered, and hurried out to the minibus. He wished he had never come on the rotten trip, certainly wished he'd never seen the stuff on Alan. Why was he so sure Alan would get him back on this one?

It took him three days. Paul noticed his bag wasn't quite where he'd left it when they came out of the library. You had to leave bags outside so people didn't swipe the reference books or the new paperbacks. He'd left his bag next to Anthony's but when they collected them at the end of English his was slightly apart. It felt different too, slightly heavier but of course that was only in hindsight. At the time he'd just picked it up and moved off. So it wasn't until registration that afternoon when Mr Campbell was calling their names that he even thought about it.

'Listen, 9C. I'm pretty upset with at least one of you, and frankly disgusted. Campbell surveyed the rows of innocent faces apparently looking for signs of guilt. He frowned and continued, 'As much as I hate to act like a policeman, on this occasion I may have to. The librarian informed me at lunch time that four brand new fantasy adventure books had gone missing from the library after this class was in there for period 4. Your English teacher is pretty angry about the whole thing – as am I. Everyone kindly empty your bags.'

To groans and protests, the content of bags were spewed out onto the desks for Mr Campbell to see. A kind of sixth sense told Paul, in a flash, what was odd about his bag – he knew what he would find before he looked. And he knew that somehow Alan was behind it. In despair he reached down the side-pocket and felt the books, all four of them. Mr Campbell was less than an aisle away and there was no time to put them anywhere else. He couldn't even be bothered.

Anthony's face dropped when he saw Paul's shaking hand deposit the books on his desk. He gawped, speechless. Paul answered his unspoken question with raised palms. The boy understood and sympathised.

He would support Paul, whatever. Mr Campbell was clearly amazed to find the books with Paul. He swept them up in his hand and dismissed the class at once, as if to protect him from further embarrassment.

'I hope this is going to be good, Paul,' he said as he settled back in his chair. 'Anthony, we don't need you here.'

'But Sir, I can prove Paul didn't steal the books.'

'How?'

'I was sitting next to him all through English and he wasn't reading them. I can tell you what he was reading.'

'And you didn't see him collect these books?'

'No Sir.'

'So how did they get there, Paul?'

'I don't know.'

'You'll have to do better than that, lad,' Mr Campbell said, almost gently.

At that moment Miss Sneed, their English teacher arrived. She took in the situation and shook her head tragically at Paul. 'Well, well, who would have thought it?'

Suddenly galvanised into his own defence, Paul burst out, 'It wasn't me, it was Alan.'

'Oh, come on now,' Miss Sneed protested. 'Don't just accuse someone else.'

'It was Alan!'

'Why do you think that?' Mr Campbell interjected.

'Because...' Paul bit his lip, afraid to go on. He daren't mention the other thing. How could he? There was no proof now, anyway. He finished lamely, '... because he doesn't like me... because of Anthony.'

'Oh, so it's Anthony's fault now, is it? It'll be my fault next for putting temptation in your way!' Miss

Sneed could be very caustic when it suited her. She took the books and clasped them to her vast bosom as if they belonged to her personally and glowered down at Paul. 'Your parents will be informed in writing of this incident. No doubt Mr Staines will be inviting them in for a chat. It will certainly be on file in your school record and the librarian may wish to bar you from using the library. Thank you, Mr Campbell.' She swept out, her stiletto heels snick-snacking up the corridor.

'I didn't do it,' Paul said, tears of frustration pricking his eyes.

Mr Campbell shuffled with papers while Paul collected himself. Anthony shovelled the books back into his friend's bag and left the room.

'I believe you, Paul,' Mr Campbell said, 'but Miss Sneed clearly doesn't and if you want me to persuade her I'm going to need a whole lot more to go on than the fact that Alan doesn't like you.'

Cornered and desperate, Paul poured out everything: finding the drugs, Sharon, the other Year 10 pupils. Alan had deliberately set him up, he was sure of it, and he didn't care what happened to him now. When he had finished, Mr Campbell patted him on the shoulder and said he'd see what he could do.

'Will my parents be told?' Paul asked.

'Not if I can intercept that letter. Whether you choose to tell them about all this is up to you. You seem to be in the way of trouble on all sides at the moment, don't you?' Campbell sympathised.

'But I haven't *done* anything,' Paul said.

'You have, I'm afraid. It's the price you have to pay for doing something when most people would do nothing.'

'Then it's much better to do nothing,' Paul murmured, disgruntled.

'Easier, but not better – I hope you'll remember that,' Mr Campbell said seriously.

'If no one blows the whistle on the minority of kids in this school dabbling with drugs, then soon Year 7 will be trying it and sooner or later someone's going to end up dead. We've all read the newspapers but pretending it doesn't exist, as some people would like, doesn't help anyone.'

'What will happen to Sharon and the rest?'

'That's not your problem anymore. Mr Staines will deal with it as he deems best. I shouldn't worry – it doesn't come as any surprise. Most of the staff have had their suspicions for a long time.'

'Why didn't you all do something before, then?'

'It's tricky. We can't go around accusing people without proof.'

Paul raised an eyebrow, all too aware of the irony of that statement. So Sharon and her cronies could get away with anything while he, a mere Year 9, could be accused of theft at the drop of a hat!

Mr Campbell smiled wearily. 'I know it all seems crazy, but I'm afraid life's like that at times.'

All the time these days, Paul thought, as he and Anthony trudged off to double Maths. He was beginning to hate school.

When he got home, Paul tried to explain to his mum what had happened but she went predictably ballistic and sent him to his room until his dad got home. His reaction was to get straight on the phone to Mr Staines to fix an early appointment.

'Why treat *me* as if I've done something wrong?' Paul demanded, when he was finally allowed downstairs for supper.

'First fights, now drugs!' his mother wailed, as she prodded bacon in the pan viciously.

'Drugs have got nothing to do with me!' Paul shouted, banging knives and forks on the table crossly.

'Don't shout at your mother,' his dad put in mildly from behind the evening paper.

'Right, that's it!' Paul announced, slamming the salt and pepper pot on the kitchen table. 'The next time I see an old lady being mugged, I'll cross over the road and pretend I didn't see it. Perhaps that'll make you happy.'

'Don't be silly, Paul,' his mum said.

'Me?' Paul was speechless.

'What I want to know,' Dad observed, 'is why we're always the last to hear about your exploits.'

'Because I can predict exactly what your reaction will be,' Paul replied wearily, 'and you seem to think I go around looking for trouble.'

Mum remained tight-lipped but her expression clearly suggested that *that* was exactly what she thought.

'If you really want to know, it's *your* fault all this has happened,' Paul added crossly.

'Mine?' It was his mother's turn to look speechless. A piece of bacon dangled precariously from the fish slice poised in her hand, as she spun round to face him.

'Yes, because if you hadn't insisted on me making friends with Anthony then Alan and I would never have fallen out in the first place.'

'It seems to me that it's a good job you're *not* hanging round with Alan if he's mixed up with drugs.

It just confirms what I've always suspected about the boy.'

'Well, it's easy to say that *now*.'

'Sheila, are we eating that bacon or are you decorating the floor with it?'

'How can you *eat* when our son is up to his ears in drug abuse and petty thieving?' his wife said, turning her accusations onto her husband.

'Well, I don't want to see your efforts go to waste, my love, otherwise believe me, I couldn't touch a thing.'

No one enjoyed the meal. His father probably would have done if it hadn't been over-cooked, but Paul and his mother picked at theirs and chased it around the plate a few times before relegating it to the bin.

Anthony phoned shortly after nine to say that he'd been down to the canal and the swans were still okay. Paul felt glad but reflected that, compared to his present problems, swans had a pretty easy time of it. What were a few bullets to the kind of aggravation he was subjected to?

When Anthony said bye, Paul felt guilty about his comments. There was no doubt about it, Anthony was a far better friend that Alan had ever been. After he'd protected him about the drugs, how could Alan go and play a dirty trick like the books on him? So why did he still wish, in his heart of hearts, that Anthony hadn't come along to tip the apple cart?

He went to bed feeling morose and as if no one in the world understood him. He and his mum seemed to be drifting further and further apart. She expected him to stand up for himself and then, when he did, she didn't like that either! It was a no-win situation.

Dad just treated everything as a joke. Paul never knew when he was being serious. He pulled the duvet over his head to blot out the lot of them.

Things at school were sorted out, after a fashion. Miss Sneed made a stiff little apology, and informed Paul that he was welcome to use the library as before. Big deal. He would be in there at every opportunity. His father and Staines drank coffee together for over half an hour and to mutual satisfaction. There was no major drugs problem, Staines assured him, and the culprits would be hunted down. He was also convinced that investigations could be carried out discreetly. Paul was wheeled in to hear Staines assure him and his father that there would be no repercussions. Paul listened with amazement as his father nodded and exchanged pleasantries with Staines as if they'd been bosom pals all their lives.

Didn't these two adults realise that the school grape-vine was far more sophisticated than they could possibly imagine? The fact that he was in the Head's office right now would have tongues wagging all over school. It wouldn't take long for Sharon and her cronies to find out who'd grassed them up. Staines didn't know what discreet meant. He was so subtle he'd probably make an announcement in assembly. 'Would all the drug users and dealers kindly meet me outside my office at lunch time? Paul Evett, 9C, will identify you at that time.' Paul Evett, 9C, dead meat.

'There you go, son, all settled,' his dad said, as they parted at the main entrance. He even ruffled his newly gelled hair. The blonde spikes didn't move but his dad came away with a sticky palm. Serve him right. Someone might have seen!

'Worse than girls, you lot these days,' he muttered,

wiping the gel off on his handkerchief. 'You'll be using make-up next. See you later.'

'Yes, Dad.' Probably not. Probably he'd have his head kicked in good and proper now. And his mum would think that was his own fault too.

5

Over the next week, Paul learned all over again what it felt like to be an outsider and a victim. Mr Staines' glib promises to his father may have been sincerely meant, but adults had no idea what kids could do without physically bullying. Worse still, Sharon and her cronies continued at school as if nothing had happened. Alan received two detentions for the book-planting trick but that was all it was judged to be – a trick.

Paul's classmates thought he'd been a bit wet to drag his father into school to moan about it. They had no idea, and really, despite Staines saying they'd flush out the drug dealers, Paul reckoned he didn't really want to find any. It suited him to let a few hints find their way to the right ears, but the last thing the Head needed was a scandal in the papers just when new parents were making choices of schools for the next September.

The result was that Paul became known as a

dobber, and the dabbling in drugs simply drifted off the school site again for a while. Paul didn't know if Alan still used the stuff or not. Probably not. All his rubbish about going out with Sharon had been a fairy story. He'd paid her for the stuff just to act big. At least he'd had a fright over that, but you'd never have guessed it looking at him. His big mouth never stopped these days. Anthony came in for a share of it but mostly Alan preferred to needle Paul. It was worst in the lessons like French and Art where Anthony was in a different group. On those occasions, Paul had no one to sit next to and he was taunted and mocked mercilessly by the gang, always under Alan's direction.

Three times in Art, one of the gang hid or swiped the object he'd selected the lesson before for still life sketching. Mrs Adams was understanding at first, but when it kept happening she became frustrated and thought Paul was deliberately being disorganised. Then they moved on to portraits and had to bring in a photograph of a friend to copy. It was nearly impossible to watch his bag all the time, so Paul was disgusted but not really surprised to find it had been rifled yet again. In Art he went to fetch the photo he'd selected, only to find a crude golliwog caricature in its place. Before he could screw it up, Mrs Adams swooped down on him and snatched it out of his hand.

'I am absolutely appalled!' she shrieked. 'I wouldn't have believed this possible of you, Paul. Go and stand outside.'

Paul was sickened. He'd had enough. He couldn't even be bothered to explain any more. For the first time in his life, Paul decided to play truant. He walked up the Art corridor, through the double doors and out. A quick doubled-up dash under the Maths block windows and he was at the back of the staff room. A hundred yards later and he was out of the school gates. Easy. Of course, he couldn't go home – Mum only worked part-time – but it was nice enough to sit on the canal bank and watch the swans. If anyone said anything, he'd say he had a dental appointment.

At the time, he just felt a huge relief. Of course he'd get in trouble later but so what? He was in trouble all the time at the moment and he'd rather sit through a few detentions with a teacher than face double French with the gang. The phrase 'between a rock and a hard place' leapt to mind.

It was easier than he'd ever imagined. He had to go and see Mrs Adams but she was surprisingly sympathetic and even said she appreciated why he'd felt so upset that he'd gone to sit in the loos! No other teacher that afternoon had noticed he was missing. With a bit of skill, Paul had a system going where he was regularly missing the odd French, Art and even some PE lessons without it ever appearing on the register. Alan knew of course, but it seemed as if he was biding his time, or maybe even *he* couldn't bring himself to drop someone in it for bunking off.

Paul went all over the place: down to the canal, round the shops, to the park. If any teacher had asked him how to stop truanting in school, he'd have been able to give them a dozen suggestions straight off. He felt a few qualms about his mum and dad when they found out and, oddly, about Mr Campbell too. Paul knew he'd be disappointed. The thing was, he couldn't stop Alan picking on him. At least being out of his reach, if only temporarily, was a relief from the constant niggling.

It was Anthony who finally confronted him when they were down at the canal together one evening a couple of weeks later. Anthony was pensive and quiet, his brown eyes moody as he gazed over the still water.

'What's on your mind?' Paul asked, rolling over onto his stomach.

'My mum.'

'What's up with her?'

'She's fed up. Wants to move back to Birmingham.'

Paul sat up. 'Would you move back?' The thought that he might be utterly friendless was just about the last straw.

Anthony shrugged. 'Dad's new job is going really well but Mum's dead miserable.'

'Why?'

'No one will talk to her in the neighbourhood, you know, or in the shops.'

'Why not?' The words were out before Paul could stop himself.

Anthony gave him a little cynical smile. 'People aren't actually rude to her or anything, they just don't talk. The neighbours haven't invited us round for coffee or anything. I mean, who cares really? But my mum does. Dad says it's because we're new. She reckons it's because we're black.'

Paul winced. He always felt uncomfortable and ashamed when Anthony made those kind of statements, so matter of fact and up front. He thought carefully before saying anything else. There was no point being dismissive, because Anthony was right. Some people *were* racist around here. Look at Gran, for starters. His parents weren't, but then they weren't exactly typical. You could never tell, just by looking at people, what they were really like inside or how they'd behave to other folk.'

'Still, you can't just move without making a go of it,' Paul said.

'I'd rather stay. It's nicer here than in the middle of Birmingham. We had more friends there, though.'

'Black friends?'

'Black and white. It's a lot more mixed up – everyone gets on more or less. I suppose they have to.'

Paul felt sorry for Anthony's mum. He could sympathise with her sense of isolation.

'Still, you can't give up, can you? She ought to keep making an effort to settle here, what with your dad's job and you.'

Anthony gave him a sly look. 'You're a good one to talk about buckling down.'

'What do you mean?' Paul was guarded.

'Well, you can't talk about not running away. How many lessons have you skived off now, or have you lost count?'

'Who told you?'

'Everyone knows! You must be mad.'

'Yeah, well, you don't know what it's like being bullied by Alan and that lot.'

'I thought they were your big buddies.'

'So did I,' Paul laughed, without humour.

'Still, you can't just give in to them.'

Paul glowered and started picking grasses out of the tow-path. He found the thick stemmed ones with the brown and cream heads and remembered firing them like little popper guns when he was a kid. He bent the stem and twisted it round the head, which popped off and hit Anthony on the forehead.

'Kid!'

'Wish I still was, sometimes.' He fired another

flower head, imagining it was real and Alan's smirking face was at the receiving end.

'You could thump him.'

'And the rest of the gang? I don't think so.'

'Beat them at their own game then.'

'What, go around playing his stupid pathetic pranks? Do me a favour. Anyway he'd just try another stunt like the books. I can't win.'

'So you'll just bunk off until the end of term?'

'Why not?'

'You'll get caught.'

'And get a load of detentions. Big deal.'

'Your grades will be rubbish, just before you decide your options for next year. That's really bright!'

'How come you're so full of wisdom, Mr Preacher?'

'It's just common sense. I'd never let Alan and that lot do that to me.'

'Do what?'

'Turn me into such a wimp that I'd fail my exams rather than stand up to them.'

Paul was stung into an angry retort. 'It was sticking up for you that got me into Alan's bad books in the first place,' he shouted crossly.

'I know.' Anthony diffused the situation by calmly accepting the blame. Paul was mortified by his own selfish, petty spite.

'I know exactly what you did – that's why I admired you so much, but I don't want you to muck up your whole education just for me. If it's so difficult for you, then ditch me and get in with Alan again.'

'I wouldn't do that!' Paul was horrified at the suggestion.

'You can't keep on doing this either,' Anthony pointed out.

'All right, stop going on. Who do you think you are – my mum?'

'Just an interested observer.'

'You realise what'll happen as soon as I stop bunking off? Someone'll realise how many times I've been away.'

'Maybe you could forge a couple of notes from your mum?' Anthony said doubtfully.

Paul looked at him in disbelief. If his mum ever found out he'd forged her signature, he'd be begging to do detentions rather than go home and face the tongue-lashing.

'I meant what I said about facing up to Alan, though,' Anthony continued, as they walked home together, swiping the heads off brambles with sticks.

'I'm not a fighter.'

'I didn't mean fists. We can use brains.'

'What, challenge him to a game of chess? Come off it!'

'No, not chess but something that means a lot to him and the gang. Something, that'll *have* to make them respect you.'

'What happened to the "we"?' Paul said archly.

'I meant "us", of course, but you know him and you'll know what he'd bite at.'

Paul shrugged. He couldn't think of anything except football and you couldn't challenge Alan at that. He was good. Paul might be better but Anthony... he'd be better off sticking to tiddly-winks. No, it needed to be something more personal. He'd have to give it some thought.

When they got back to Paul's home, his mum was still at work. He remembered she was doing holiday cover for someone and wouldn't be in until six. A twinge of remorse made him start the washing-up while Anthony fixed drinks for them both. He glanced at the letters which his mum had stuffed behind the clock, unopened, in her rush to get out of the house that morning. With a stomach-turning wrench he recognised the school logo on one of them.

He wiped the suds off and fingered the envelope with trembling hands. He really didn't need any more aggravation just now. He'd decided not to play truant any more. So there was no harm in taking the letter, was there? He jammed it in his pocket just as he heard his mum's key in the lock.

'Hi, love! Oh, that's good of you,' she said, survey-ing the washing up with obvious pleasure. Paul red-dened and felt even guiltier that she was so pleased about even the smallest bit of help he offered.

'Hello, Anthony. How are you? Your parents OK?'

'Yes thanks.'

'Good, I must get round to inviting them over soon. Do they both work?'

'Only my dad.'

'So what would be a good evening do you think, for me to invite them over for a meal?'

Anthony looked pleased and embarrassed at the same time. 'Any evening really. Mum doesn't go out much and Dad's in about half-six most days.'

'Well, let's say Friday, then. Will you ask them or should I phone?'

'I'll ask tonight.'

'Don't forget now, I know what you boys are like,' she threatened teasingly.

Paul could have hugged her. He'd been thinking all the way home about persuading her to ask Anthony's mum round and she'd beaten him to it. Now Anthony would know it wasn't just because he'd said how his mum felt and it would mean even more. She really was okay, for a mother. He felt the crumpled letter sticking into his thigh through his trouser pocket. A strong impulse to take the letter out and put it in her hand nearly overcame him but he fought it down. Just in case weakness should confuse him again, he took the opportunity of her going to the freezer in the garage to rip it up without reading it and toss it in the bin. What she didn't know wouldn't hurt her, he told himself in justification. He still felt bad about it though, even hours later when he was tossing and turning, hot and sticky in bed.

The days until Friday were a nightmare. French was doubly difficult because he'd missed so many important bits. The module they were now on was a complete mystery. Alan's jibes seemed almost trivial compared to the teacher's constant nagging about why he didn't know this, that or the other verb ending. He was cribbing notes off anyone he could persuade or bribe and furiously copying up every evening so his exercise books didn't show too many blanks. Even so, his grades had slipped horribly and he kept expecting another letter in the post so he was up before his mum every day, ostensibly making tea, but in reality intercepting the postman. At least there had been no repercussions about that other letter yet and Paul stopped feeling so bad about throwing it away. Nobody could say he wasn't working now. He didn't have time for anything else.

The swans' remaining eggs had hatched at last and the four cygnets were growing at an amazing rate. The boys felt more secure now that the female was less of a sitting target but they still kept up their watch.

Anthony was able to help Paul's return to school in two ways. For a start he wangled a move into Art, claiming that Music just wasn't his strong point. Nobody who'd heard him sing could deny that and, as luck would have it, group numbers worked in his favour so that a swap could be made. Paul had always liked Art and even though Anthony was no better at it than Music, what he could ensure was that Alan and the others left Paul alone. In fact, although he wasn't exactly macho or tough, he was a lot more streetwise than the others. At least, some of the girls seemed to think so, not least Karen. She had started to talk to him in tutor time and that resulted in the second favour Anthony was able to do Paul. She lent Anthony her French notes for the entire term, including all the homework Paul had missed.

He wouldn't have dared ask her. Actually he'd always considered her a bit thick but he soon discovered his error. The notes were neat, much clearer than his own, with useful little rules jotted in the margin. At last the dreaded module started to make sense.

If there was one thing he'd learned this term it was that stopping bunking off was a lot more difficult than starting. He could see now why some Year 11 kids who did it ended up dropping out of exams altogether. Paul promised himself he'd never be so stupid again. The few hours off were never worth all this back-breaking sweat to catch up.

Friday evening couldn't come soon enough. For one thing, Paul could stop running just to stand still, and for another, Mum had been cooking since Wednesday for her dinner party. She'd invited their neighbours the Rogers, who were really nice, so that the Ahmeds had someone else to meet. So the only fly in the ointment was Gran, who'd more or less demanded an invite. She was bringing her home-made sherry trifle which was a bonus because Gran was not in the habit of just showing her trifle the sherry bottle. As a little kid Paul had once been squiffy on two helpings of the stuff. On the down-side, could she be trusted not to put her foot in it where the Ahmeds were concerned?

Fortunately when it came to it, Gran was completely bowled over by Mr Ahmed taking her arm and sitting her down at the dining table. So much so, and a couple of glasses of wine later, that by the end of the evening she had pronounced them the most decent couple she'd ever met and what a difference to some of the riff-raff coming into the neighbourhood.

The Rogers from next door were cheerful and kind, as they always were, but Paul was really pleased to see his mum jabbering away to Mrs Ahmed and his dad listening to Mr Ahmed talking about his computer firm with real interest. His dad hated dinner parties but he was making a mammoth effort and coming across as the perfect host. Paul felt proud of them both. They might embarrass and annoy him some of the time but when it mattered they came up trumps. He could even forgive the open-toed sandals tonight. Well, he was in the privacy of his own home.

He and Anthony slipped up to Paul's room while the adults moved on to coffee in the lounge and some hideous music from the seventies which they managed to drown out with some more suited to their tastes.

'This'll make all the difference to my mum, you know,' Anthony said.

'I hope so, she's nice. Once my mum starts introducing her to people she'll be out all over the place.'

'They were talking about going to church on the way over here.'

'Well, they could go along with us.'

'They went a bit in Birmingham but I never went.'

'Why not?'

'I don't believe in that stuff. Do you?'

'Well... yes, I do.'

'It's okay as a kind of social club I suppose,' Anthony conceded, loading up one of the disks ready for a game. 'You can leave out all the "Jesus Saves with the Woolwich" rubbish though.'

'You can't do that,' Paul groaned.

'What?'

'Just dismiss it. Don't you ever think about all those people all over the world sitting in churches, praying and that.'

'So?'

'It's weird, kind of, I mean, don't you reckon if they were *all* wasting their time someone would know?'

'All the people washing their cars and going shopping on Sunday probably reckon they're right.'

'But I bet if there was a war or something like a killer plague, they'd all be rushing off to church too, just in case.'

'Maybe. So you go as a kind of insurance do you, against bad luck?'

'No, it's not that. I've never had more bad luck than I have in the past few weeks,' Paul exclaimed stabbing the level six button.

'What's the point of going then?'

'I think it's a place where people can trust each other a bit more than they usually do, because they're trying to live in a way which pleases God. They try to have more respect for each other.'

'Back to the social club theory.'

'No, because it's to do with God, as well. God is bigger, more important than themselves.'

'Do you believe in God?'

'Yes,' Paul hesitated, checking his thoughts. 'Yes, I do.' He felt confident now. It was a strange but good feeling that the world wasn't just a mish-mash of lives and events hurling aimlessly along, but that there was a plan for everyone and some meaning in it all. God was in control but you had to choose which way you went. He hadn't consciously thought about it much but just recently a lot of things were *having* to be thought about.

'Hey, did you get that letter signed up for taster week in the summer?'

'What letter?'

'The one the Head sent home for all Year 9. You must have had one. You get to try six option subjects and then pick four for next year. First come first served though. I got mine done ages ago.'

'Mine must have got lost in the post,' Paul said slowly. He couldn't believe his own stupidity sometimes. If only he'd bothered to open the blasted letter. If only he hadn't taken it in the first place...

'Are you playing then or what?'

'Sure,' Paul said and gunned down eight alien attackers in a frenzied blast of ammo which made him feel only fractionally better. God would be having a good old laugh about that one at any rate.

They were up to level twenty before Paul's mum called for them to come down and say goodbye to the Rogers. It was gone eleven but it looked as if everyone had enjoyed themselves. The Ahmeds stayed for one more cup of coffee and Mum was talking about her job at the dental surgery where she was a receptionist and in charge of clients' records and accounts. Mrs Ahmed looked all flustered but kind of excited too, especially when Paul's mum said they needed another part-timer in the autumn.

'Now Sheila, stop organising people's lives. Maybe Alec doesn't want his wife working.'

'I'm sure Alec wouldn't be so mean as to stop Susan doing something which might get her more involved in the community,' his wife returned, giving Alec little choice except to agree.

Paul had to hand it to his mum – she could be clever and she understood people. It was clear to anyone that Susan wanted to work but didn't have much confidence. Maybe having a husband with such a high-powered job made you feel a bit inadequate. And being black in an all-white community would more or less cap it all. But his mum was talking about getting her an application form and taking her down to meet the dental staff, as if there was no obstacle to her getting the job, if she wanted. It suddenly gave him an idea about how to deal with Alan and his gang. If his mum could gently manipulate people for their own good then maybe he could too.

The next day he decided to act while he still had the courage to face Alan. They were together in French first thing and instead of sitting alone as usual, Paul went over to his desk and sat down. He ignored the snide comments and sniggers for a while and then turned on Alan while the teacher was giving out books over the far side of the room.

'Don't say another word unless you want to back it up, right?'

Alan was wrong-footed. 'Are you asking for a fight?'

'If you like.'

'You and whose army?'

'Anthony's pretty handy. He's black belt,' Paul lied, calling his bluff. 'But that's not what we had in mind.'

'What then?'

'Kind of contest.'

'Alan's eyes flickered maliciously but there was a spark of interest in their icy depths.

'Go on,' he drawled.

'A series of games, challenges if you like. You and whoever from the gang, against me and Anthony.'

'What's in it?

'If Anthony and I win...'

'Which you won't.'

'...if we do, you cut out all the aggro. No more messing with either of us – ever.'

Alan's upper lip curled in a derisory sneer. 'Getting too much for the jungle bunny, is it?'

'No,' Paul returned evenly, controlling his temper, 'it's just boring and I thought you might like to play for higher stakes than a bit of playground bullying, at your age.' He watched that last dig sink in and hoped he hadn't overstepped the mark.

'What's in it for me, then, assuming I decide to play?'

'Five quid a week for the rest of this term.'

'Each,' Alan snapped back.

Paul hesitated. This was ridiculous. They would struggle to raise five quid, ten was out of the question. Alan saw the uncertainty and pushed home his advantage. 'Ten or forget it, and the hassle goes on.'

'Agreed.'

'Now, for the challenge. What will it be?'

'Each person chooses one game. Points system.'

'Okay. Scott'll be with me. We'll have 1500 metres running.'

'Computers – our choice of game.'

'Pool', Alan countered.

'Cycling – cross-country.'

It was out before Paul had time to think. His brain was doing somersaults trying to work out the odds he'd given them. Pool – dead loss. He and Anthony were complete duffers while Alan played all the time at his dad's work's club. Scott regularly won at 1500 metres. He felt confident on computers but the cycling... daft choice – Scott probably trained doing that.

'Two weeks for preparation and a truce until then,' he added, buying some time.

'Payments back-dated for those weeks.'

'If you win,' Paul conceded.

'Oh, we'll win!' Alan cooed. He was loving this. Paul wished he'd said boxing and could have landed one right in the middle of Alan's stupid piggy nose. Strange how these violent urges kept coming over him. He turned away with a nod and sat through the first peaceful lesson he'd had for as long as he could remember. By break the lower school corridor was buzzing with the news. A bit unfortunate, considering that Paul hadn't had time to break the news to Anthony yet. Well, it *had* been his idea really, so that part wouldn't be a shock. Knowing he was favourite to lose a fiver a week for eight weeks might be, though...

6

'You really are an idiot sometimes,' Anthony exclaimed.

'What choice did I have?' Paul protested. 'I thought you'd be pleased – it *was* your idea.'

'Pleased that I'm going to be the victim of an extortion racket – organised courtesy of my so-called best friend?' Anthony was incredulous.

'We just might win,' Paul objected hopefully, but not with a lot of conviction.

'Pigs might fly an' all.'

'Listen, we've got two weeks to prepare.'

'You've enlisted a few celebrities to coach us, have you? Linford Christie dropping in later, I suppose!'

'I'll admit they've probably got the edge on us as far as the running goes, but we've still got the computer contest...'

'Yes and the cycling! Whatever possessed you... I mean, we haven't even got decent bikes! I bet those two will turn up with twenty-seven gear jobs and we'll be eating their dust round the entire course. Where *is* the course, by the way?'

'Up on the moor somewhere,' Paul replied, vaguely. He didn't want to go into too many details. It was a tough course and pretty wet. Anthony didn't need to know about that.

'Anyway, I think we'll be all right on the computer bit,' Paul said confidently, changing tack onto more positive thoughts.

'One out of four still sounds like a fiver a week I owe.'

'Look, I meant to talk to you about that. I'll pay the tenner, whatever happens.'

'What will you use for money?'

'I'll get a job. Do two paper-rounds, something like that.'

'Don't be daft. We're in this together. If we lose, and let's face it, we're *going* to lose, then we'll have to get through the next eight weeks somehow. Hey, maybe I can win a bit on the arcades.'

Paul frowned and looked at his toes.

'All right, I know you disapprove of that, so I'll have to get a paper round too – or maybe I could extend my gardening talents!'

Paul had to laugh, despite the gloom which was rapidly descending. It had all seemed like such a brilliant idea yesterday, whereas now it seemed worse than putting up with the bullying and waiting for Alan to grow up.

Campbell got wind of the challenge by the end of the day and spoke to Paul the next morning in registration. He was clearly worried and threatening to put an embargo on the whole thing.

'I've heard some of the tutor group saying you're

taking bets on who will win.'

'That's not true, Sir.'

'Well, I hope not, because I'm not allowing gambling in this tutor group, or any other come to that. And what's this I hear about you paying money if you lose? It all sounds highly irregular, especially coming from you, Paul.'

Paul sighed. How many times had he heard that these past few weeks. He was getting tired of people expecting too much from him all the time when everyone else had excuses made for them left, right and centre. There were times when he'd just like to go and smash a few windows, indulge in a quick bit of graffiti and kick a few heads in, just to prove he wasn't any different from anyone else.

'I'm not challenging Alan for money, Sir, just for a bit of peace and quiet.'

'And when you lose, you're happy to pay for his cigarettes and whatever else he gets up to.'

'That was his forfeit, Sir. I can't argue with that when it's my challenge.'

Mr Campbell gazed across the playground thoughtfully. 'You know I can't let this happen, don't you?'

'Well, if you don't, things will just go on as before and they'll be worse because he'll say I'm a coward.'

'Is that a challenge to me?'

'No, Sir,' Paul sighed. He couldn't win these days.

'Okay, so this challenge goes ahead, but on the condition that we organise it properly and you all collect sponsorship from the tutor group and at home to put towards a good cause. At least someone will benefit from your hard efforts and there will be an impartial referee. How does that sound?'

'Thanks, Sir. That'd be brilliant,' Paul smiled shyly.

'Who will be referee, Sir?'

'Me, of course.'

Paul grinned. He knew he could trust Campbell to make sure everything was fair and square. Alan and his lot wouldn't dare cheat if Campbell was on the case.

Alan would have kicked up all kinds of fuss if anyone else had suggested the sponsorship idea but once Mr Campbell had organised proper headed sponsorship forms and a group of kids including Karen to collect names and money he was swept along with the tide like everyone else. Most of the tutor group knew what it was really about but they were willing to chip in their loose change and decided to vote for a couple of local charities to divide the cash between.

'Right then, we'll start Monday week on the athletics track for the first event, 1500 metres, to begin after last lesson. All supporters welcome,' Mr Campbell announced.

'Yeah, come and watch me win!' Scott gloated from the back row.

'What's our strategy to win this one then?' Anthony said, as they changed into running shorts that evening.

'We *can't* win,' Paul informed him simply.

'Well I think I'll just go and sit in front of the TV, if that's your attitude.'

'What I mean is, we can't win, but we can't come third and fourth either. It's a points system remember, so even if Scott wins, which he's bound to do, one of us needs to beat Alan.

Anthony did a few ludicrous high kicks on the spot. 'No problem — I'm super-fit. Phew, actually I think I've just pulled something.'

'Stop clowning around and get running — it's four

times round the track.'

'Four times! You've got to be joking, man.'

'Come on,' Paul called back over his shoulder. I'll pace you.'

Anthony's reply was lost in the wind. Paul grinned, put his head down and tried to forget everything except running. He was just aware of Anthony pounding at his heels and kept the pace reasonably easy. Scott would be haring round like a greyhound but there wasn't any point in depressing Anthony yet. He wanted to make sure they could both actually complete the distance without having heart attacks.

Four circuits later they collapsed on the verge, lungs on fire and legs weak.

'Phew! I never realised I was so unfit,' Anthony gasped, flicking beads of sweat out of his eyes. 'You're going to kill me, you and your daft challenges.'

'Right, do you want the good news or the bad?'

'Give me the good first.'

'Well, we've got over a week to improve.'

'And the bad?'

Paul consulted his watch. 'Scott regularly turns in a time beating ours by about a minute.'

'A minute! A whole minute!' Anthony groaned and fell back on the ground.

'It could be worse,' Paul encouraged him. 'Alan isn't anywhere near as fast.'

'But I was going flat out. Right, that's it, I'm going home to slump in front of the telly. I need a drink and food, masses of food, I'm starving.'

'Hang on a minute. We're in training try and remember.'

'Yes and I need energy, of the chocolate variety.'

'We've got to get to level thirty on the computer

tonight – there won't be time for you to eat.'

'At least that only involves moving a couple of fingers!'

All things considered, the week was a gruel and not particularly enjoyable. Neither boys were natural runners although Paul's love of football meant he was a good deal fitter. Just pounding round a track wasn't much fun though and they ended up doing more jogging around the canal than sticking to the athletics track. It wasn't quite as good practice but it was less tedious.

Alan stuck to his word for once and there were no aggravations in lessons but Paul still sensed his hostility and felt that, whatever happened, things could never be the same between them.

Before they were anywhere near properly trained, the weekend arrived and with it a phone call from Simon at the youth club asking if Paul could referee a junior match on Saturday morning.

'No way, Anthony and I are training,' Paul answered, when his mum gave him the message.

She shrugged. 'Well, it's up to you, but tell him so yourself. I'm not doing your dirty work for you.'

Grumbling, Paul dropped his running trainers at the front door and went to the phone. 'Now I suppose I'll be made to feel like a completely mean git,' he muttered, stabbing numbers on the phone crossly.

Mum remained silent as she dolloped cake mixture into a tin. Susan Ahmed had given her the special saffron recipe and she was trying it for the first time.

'Hello, is Simon in? ... Oh, well can you give him a message? I can't ...' Paul watched the slight stiffening of his mum's shoulders as she listened to his side of the conversation. Why did she always have to judge him like that, without saying anything? Why did he have to be Superman all over the place? 'It's all right. Just say I can do the refereeing. I'll see him there. Bye.'

He replaced the receiver and watched his mum scraping the bowl. She turned to hand him the gooey spoon, which was still liberally coated with the cake mixture. Paul took it with a little smile and licked it appreciatively. Ah well, they were going to lose anyway. A couple more runs wouldn't help so he might as well give the little kids his time.

'Thanks, love,' Mum said. 'I would've been disappointed if you'd said no.'

'Why do I always have to do the right thing by everybody?'

'I'm sorry if it seems a terrible burden,' she teased.

'Yes, it does sometimes. Look at this daft contest thing ...'

'That was your solution, Paul. We could have dealt with it in other ways, I could have spoken to Alan's mum. She knows what her son is like.'

Paul shook his head. 'You don't understand, Mum. It wouldn't have worked. I had to stand up for myself. Everyone does in the end. I've hated this term.'

'I know. You've grown up an awful lot though.'

'Is that a good thing?'

'Inevitable. At least you're not beating around in Alan's wake all the time.'

'No, now I'm at loggerheads with him all the time. Big improvement!'

'In the long run it will be, you'll see, and in the meantime don't turn your back on all the other people around you.'

'Like the junior youth team! That'll be a bundle of laughs.'

'You'll make their day, at any rate.'

'And who's going to make *mine*? That's what I'd like to know.'

Mum dunked her mixing bowl down under the tap and squirted washing liquid at it. 'You don't do things looking for a reward or a pay back. If we're Christians we aim to live like Christ did – to serve others. We don't do it just to feel good, though that may be a result. You'll probably feel good about yourself when you give those kids a good game. That's something Alan's never felt in his life because he can't be anything except selfish. He's the one I feel sorry for because he'll grow up into a discontented man who'll never believe he's had anything.'

Paul picked up his trainers and untied the laces. He couldn't quite see things like that but maybe his mum was right about Alan not being really happy. Paul always thought he had everything, had envied him for years, but just recently he'd thought more and more that he didn't want to be like Alan. For one thing, outside of the gang he wasn't very popular. He just had clout but that wasn't quite the same thing.

Paul called round at Anthony's house briefly and left him on level thirty-five, their highest ever, promising to be back as soon as the match ended. He jogged down there and spent half an hour getting some order into the mayhem which greeted him. They had to grab a kid off the mini assault course to make up numbers and the array of colours was so confusing that Paul decided they'd better play skins versus shirts or he'd never have a clue. They kicked off at half past ten to cheers from the thin band of supporters, mostly mums and dads and a youth with a dog who kept running off with the ball.

Simon the curate arrived for half-time with orange juice and biscuits. He looked a bit hassled and apologised for being late but he was clearly very grateful for Paul's help. They chatted briefly about the contest and Paul found himself confiding some of the details about how it all began. He was very serious about it and said that, while he couldn't help much, he did have a pool table in his study at home and could give them a game or two if that would help.

'Do you play a lot then?' Paul queried.

'Well, let's say I used to.'

'Where?'

'Pubs and clubs. The usual. I wasn't always a vicar or even thinking about being one, you know!'

Paul had always imagined vicars were born in dog collars and with smiles fixed on their faces. He couldn't quite see Simon swigging ale and potting balls. They needed any help going, though. Gratefully he accepted Simon's offer of a few games after church on Sunday morning and made a mental note to get Anthony there as well.

After that it was back to the game. He began to realise how Mr Parr felt when half a dozen screaming players started appealing for handball and accusing him of diminished vision. Taking charge, he indicated 'play on' and refused to be moved by the one or two insistent hecklers. Once that was established, the game began to look less like a rag-tag session. Paul blew the final whistle on a three-two win for the church side, satisfied that he'd done his best. A couple of parents shook his hand at the end and thanked him for sparing the time. That, and the excitement on the faces of both teams, made Paul glad that he'd spared the time and made the effort. Mum had been right.

He'd got far too wound up in his own plans to even think about other people.

Anthony was a bit reluctant to go to church but he finally agreed and turned up with his parents. Susan Ahmed looked happier and far less nervous than when Paul had first met her. Still very shy, she looked pleased when people came to talk to her, and thanks partly to Paul's mum, plenty did. Anthony was non-committal about the service but didn't say anything critical about it, only mentioning that it had gone pretty quickly. Paul took this to mean that he hadn't been bored witless at any rate. There was a blend of old and new. The drama group did something in the service and the vicar didn't follow a specific routine. It made it more interesting, somehow.

After coffee, Simon was as good as his word, taking them into his study and explaining a few techniques to improve their potting skills. Paul raised an eyebrow at Anthony as they watched Simon cut balls into pockets from all angles, leaving the white ball perfectly placed for the next shot.

'You can't expect to improve overnight,' Simon said, as another red spun into the farthest pocket, deftly knocking the opposing yellow out in the process.

'You're brilliant!' Anthony whistled.

'Yes, well do me a favour and keep it quiet. Not everyone in church circles would approve,' he winked.

They spent a couple of hours lining up simple shots and, for the first time in Paul's experience, actually knowing where they'd end up. He still couldn't cut in to the side pockets with any degree of accuracy or understand how to snooker his opponent except by pure fluke but at least straightforward shots were going in and where they didn't he was leaving things a shade more tricky for his opponent.

'This is going to be a breeze,' Anthony bragged, smacking the black decisively into the pocket.

'We'll give them a run for their money, anyway,' Paul said, more moderately.

'Personally, I'm in favour of conceding the running and concentrating on this event.'

'No way. We're going to wipe the smiles off their faces in *every* event. Win or lose, they're going to have to fight for every point.'

'Right lads, come back tomorrow and we'll see if we can make any more improvements,' Simon said.

'Really? That's brilliant,' Paul said.

'Oh, and good luck with the run after school.'

'Thanks.'

'He's all right, for a vicar,' Anthony said as they wandered home together.

Monday wasn't a bad day usually, but Paul was on tenterhooks all the time and his stomach was a knot of butterflies as they changed for the run. Practically the entire Year 9 had stayed behind to watch which made Paul feel even worse. They limbered up and tried to look confident despite their sinking spirits.

'I'm last, I know I'm last,' Anthony kept repeating until Paul felt so jangled he told him to shut up.

'What's our plan, then?' Anthony wittered on in his ear.

Paul watched Alan and tried to work out their best approach. Finally, he just told Anthony to run like hell and finish even if he broke a leg.

'Oh great, I can see you've spent hours on the finer strategies. It's nice to know you've got so much faith in me,' Anthony said, pretending to be hurt.

'Let's face it, Anthony, you're no runner. Just don't drop out!'

'As if!'

'On your marks!' Campbell called, waving stragglers off the track.'

'Good luck, Anthony!' someone screamed from the sideline. It was Karen. Paul was amazed. He glared at Anthony, who shrugged in mock innocence and gave her the benefit of his high kick warm-up step.

'Ready – Go!'

Anthony, wrong-footed, lurched into Paul, spoiling his getaway. He was even laughing. Some help he'd be. Right, now where was Alan? In front, setting the pace for Scott whose long stride was eating up the ground. Stay with him, not ahead, just with him. The first circuit was murder. He couldn't breathe properly because he was so wound up and the pace was much faster than he was used to. He'd never keep it up. Don't think about it, don't panic, just run. He shot a quick look behind and regretted it immediately. Anthony was way back, head down with that lop-sided gangly style of his. Okay, first and fourth positions pretty well decided then. It didn't matter, it was between him and Alan. He had to beat Alan, then the scores would be more or less even. They needed this draw.

Scott surged forward as they started the third lap and left a heart-stopping gap which, mercifully, Alan slid back into. Scott was going way ahead, coasting to victory. Paul was dimly aware of the spectators yelling Scott's name. The pressure was off – they weren't really watching him. All that pelting up and down on the football field was paying off. His heartbeat steadied and he found the energy to keep slapping his feet down in the same rhythm, only now he was drawing level with Alan, or was Alan slipping behind? Whichever it was, he ploughed on, concentrating only on the shoulder of the boy beside him, determined to pass it.

For a split second both boys glanced at each other and Paul was surprised to see the pain and fear in the other's eyes. Alan who was so hard, so super-cool and powerful – he really was frightened of being beaten. It mattered. Paul fleetingly lost concentration. He saw but couldn't avoid the elbow which came up apparently wildly and caught him in the side, knocking the breath out of him and spinning him off course.

Recovering, he fought to clear his head and get back on a line as the bell for the final lap jangled discordantly in his ears. Alan wasn't going to get away with it, not this time. He saw the track ahead through a haze of red and the sound of his own blood coursing through his veins drowned out the cheers as Scott crossed the winning line. His side ached but he was oblivious to it – all he could feel was the power in his legs and the terrible rage as he pumped his feet up and down. Paul knew he could reach Alan, knew he could overtake him, he had never been more certain, and never felt more determined. With metres to go he drew level again and, with an eye to those sharp elbows, passed Alan and forged on to the finishing line. Alan collapsed on his heels, almost sobbing with frustration.

Anthony cruised in, still laughing and doing a little side-step, presumably for Karen's benefit, as he stepped daintily over the line and crashed dramatically to the ground.

'Superb race!' Campbell said, as he clapped all four lads on the shoulder and called for the spectators to give everyone air.

Paul felt waves of nausea wash over him for a couple of minutes. He couldn't have stood up to save his life but despite the dull throb in his side and the fire in the back of his throat, victory was sweet. Scott had won, and deserved to, but he'd beaten Alan. Alan who couldn't bear to be beaten, who had to cheat just in case someone was better. Nobody had seen the incident and Paul was glad. He didn't want Campbell taking his side or anyone else to know. He knew and Alan, lying there beside him on the ground, knew. His silence now was even further proof, if proof were needed, that he was more powerful on his own than Alan could ever be. Paul looked at Alan, his red puffy face and his cruel blue eyes and didn't feel threatened any more. Alan glared at him momentarily and, feeling his own inadequacy, dropped his gaze.

'Now then, working on a points system, Scott and Alan score sixteen points for first and third positions. Paul and Anthony score twelve points. Currently in the lead, Scott and Alan, but everything to play for,' Campbell announced to cheers and applause on all sides.

'Quiet please!' he ordered, raising his hands. 'Before we leave, let's set the date for the Computer play-off. Wednesday lunch time, room 2. Spectator space limited, I'm afraid, so first come first served. Right, off you go.'

The crowd filtered away, leaving only the four contestants and Campbell.

Anthony and Scott were the first to recover. The real battle of wills had been between the other two.

Alan set off with Scott as soon as he could muster enough breath to walk normally.

'Bad luck, you two,' Mr Campbell said.

'What d'you mean, Sir?' Anthony laughed. 'That was our game plan, and it worked a treat.'

'I suppose so.'

'We'll thrash them at computers, you wait and see, Sir.'

'I can't wait. All right, Paul?'

'Yes, Sir.'

'I'll mention your time to Mr Parr. I'm sure he'd be interested.'

'Oh, no thanks, Sir.'

'But you've obviously trained hard to get this far. I'm sure you could get into running.'

'I couldn't, Sir, honestly. I couldn't ever run that fast again. I wouldn't need to, you see.'

Mr Campbell gave him an odd look and then nodded. 'I see.'

Paul thought he probably did.

Elated, the boys made their way home, buoyed up by success and the anticipation of a much easier ride on Wednesday. There was every chance of them forging into the lead and, with Simon's coaching, even the pool contest looked less daunting.

'Shall we just nip down to the canal before we go home?' Paul suggested. He didn't know why, he just felt a sudden urge to go there.

'I'm starving!' Anthony protested.

'Here, have my packed lunch, I couldn't manage any.'

'You ran on an empty stomach!'

'You might have run faster if you had as well,' Paul teased.

Anthony flipped the sandwich box lid open and peered in. He made a long decision about whether to try the corned beef sandwiches or the crisps but ended up eating both.

'Hm, now I can think straight.'

'You must have hollow legs.'

'At least I'm not a stick insect like you.'

They cleared the gate and trotted down to the tow path. Oddly, at this time in the afternoon, the Warden was there. His brown face, crinkled from squinting in the early summer sunshine looked dark and ominous. He recognised the boys and walked towards them. 'Bad news, I'm afraid,' he growled. 'Sorry business all round.'

'The shooters have been back again?' Paul blurted out the question, his heart tightening uncomfortably.

'Afraid so. It's a damn shame. I thought they'd be all right with the babies hatched out and swimming but some people...' He shook his head in obvious disbelief at the wickedness of certain individuals.

'What happened?' Anthony's voice was small and squeaky.

'They've shot the male. Hole right through its wing.'

'Dead?'

'No, luckily I spotted him this morning. Must have happened yesterday some time. I got the RSPCA to get down here. A right old dance he led us but we finally caught him and strapped the wing up. So she's on her own now.'

'Will she manage without her mate?'

'As far as feeding them goes, yes, I can't see why not. It's whether they let her bring them up.'

'They?'

'The young idiots who seem set on doing away with the lot of 'em.'

Paul and Anthony looked at each other in mute helplessness. After all their efforts at protection, this seemed such a cruel blow.

The excitement of the race melted away. None of that seemed in the slightest bit important. Worst of all, the attack had happened yesterday, one of the few days they'd missed going down to see the swans. If only they'd bothered with that instead of all this stupid challenge business, perhaps the louts wouldn't have been able to hurt them again.

'Can't you just put them all in a sanctuary?' Anthony asked.

The warden shook his head. 'They're wild birds and the canal is where they belong. Sanctuaries are over-run with injured birds who can't make it on their own. It wouldn't be the answer.'

'But they'll be back, bound to.'

'Not if I can help it.'

'You can't stay out here permanently,' Paul pointed out.

'No, that's true, but I can stay till sunset tonight and in the morning I'm going to phone around and get a few volunteers to mount a watch.'

'We'll help. We've been coming most evenings,' Anthony said.

'And it hasn't worked,' Paul said.

'We can't give in to a few louts,' the warden said, turning his collar against a fresh breeze springing up.

Paul shivered. He felt sure now that keeping watch wasn't enough. Maybe more direct action was necessary.

7

'All set for the challenge tomorrow, then?' Mr Campbell asked as he gathered papers up off his desk.

Paul shrugged. Somehow it didn't seem so important any more. He'd rather be down at the canal watching out for the swan-shooters than stuck with his nose against a computer screen, trying to reach level 36 in under four hours. He hadn't touched his computer for the last two evenings and didn't feel very confident about even this, their best chance of the challenge.

'What's up?' Mr Campbell asked, more carefully. He stopped fiddling with papers and gave Paul his full attention. Paul wriggled under his gaze. The last of the class had filed out and they were alone.

'Nothing really,' he murmured but with a kind of question mark in his tone which stopped the young teacher from making the usual dismissive comments and getting along to the staff room for a much needed cup of tea. Instead, Mr Campbell sat down and waited.

'You go to church, don't you, Sir?' Paul said.

'Yes.'

'And you pray?'

'Yes, though perhaps not so often as I should.' He tried to be as honest as he could.

'Well, why? I mean, why do you pray?'

Mr Campbell looked thoughtful. 'Why do I pray or what do I pray for?'

'Both I suppose. What do you expect to happen?'

'I see what you're getting at. Well, in a way, what you expect is a matter of faith. I don't usually expect miracles to happen and you could say that's why they don't! On a world-wide basis, I try to pray for things to change for the better, for the good, and on a more personal level, I pray for help in changing things or even accepting them.'

'Have you ever thought that praying was just a waste of time?'

'I doubt there's a Christian in the world who hasn't thought that at some time. But it depends how you look at it. You don't always see instant results. And remember, prayer is a two-way process. God wants to be in a close relationship with us, and he wants us to talk to him about everything. We can't just use prayer as a shopping list, though.'

'I know that,' Paul said with a touch of frustration.

'I'm sorry, I didn't mean to be simplistic,' Mr Campbell paused, trying to gauge his response.

'Since we saw the swan eggs being destroyed, I've prayed every night for God to keep the others safe. Well, that's not selfish or unreasonable, is it? And I've tried to help out myself – you know, going down there. Then there's this business with Alan. Well, I've been friends with Anthony and I thought...'

'That God owes you one?'

It sounded childish and daft the way Campbell put it but yes, in a way, that was exactly what Paul had expected. He couldn't understand God letting him down so badly. It made him feel like giving up on everything.

'I'm sure God could have made us all automatons, all doing the right thing, caring for each other and the world. There'd be no need for rules, police, people fighting against evil. How does that sound?'

Paul grinned, 'Boring!'

'We also wouldn't have free will. Some of the best things people have done or said have been when they've been right up against it, when things have been as black as they can be. Now I'm not saying, let's all go out looking for trouble. Believe me, I'd quite like a bit of the boring part of life with everything happy and peaceful but we wouldn't be praying at all, I guess, if the whole world was perfect. The important thing is not to give up when things seem hopeless. Then you pray for new courage, strength, ideas... whatever it takes and I do believe God won't fail you in those circumstances.'

'But he can't stop yobs with guns?'

'Well he could zap them, but then he'd be taking away free will and we're back to being his robots.'

'Sounds like a bit of a cop-out,' Paul grumbled.

'Well, think about it – we can't have it all ways. You either want to choose how you think and act or you want to be totally controlled.'

'I just want *some* people controlled.'

'That's up to the rest of us, I'm afraid, but God will give us the ability to do that in spite of our weaknesses or failings...You haven't done so badly yourself.'

'I don't feel as if I ever achieve anything except getting myself into all kinds of trouble.'

'What about this challenge? The class has got really enthusiastic about it. There's over a hundred pounds in the school office to share between whatever charities you and the others choose. That's something positive to come out of this rift between you and Alan. It's also made you stand up for yourself and someone else. Isn't Anthony's friendship worth a bit of fighting for?'

'Yes of course.'

'Don't keep looking at what you *haven't* achieved; try to be thankful for the good bits of any situation. And keep praying, whatever happens. You might find God can exceed your expectations in the long run.'

Paul looked at his teacher with new respect. Campbell could be relied on, he had discovered, not to treat Paul any differently from his class-mates and yet they shared something most of the others had no idea about. It created a kind of bond which made it easier to talk to Campbell than other teachers and he knew what it was like in a school and how things worked.

'See you, Sir,' Paul shouted over his shoulder. Some of the troubles seemed to have lifted from his shoulders and he felt more cheerful with himself and the world in general.

After a hurried tea, Paul phoned Anthony to arrange their last practice session before the contest the next day. He was just on his way out when the game warden phoned, asking if Paul and Anthony were free to watch the swans that evening for a couple of hours. There was no decision to make. Of course the swans came first, but they really had needed a final session. Karen had let slip to Anthony during tutorial that Alan and Scott had managed level 30 in just over three hours at the weekend. They were probably close to Paul and Anthony's best now, if not over their limit. They might as well raid their savings accounts right now and start paying up.

An unexpected turn of events occurred however when Paul's dad arrived home. He looked weary after his day at work but when he heard about the warden's phone call he suddenly suggested a walk down there and a drink in the pub near the lock gates.

'That'll save you boys going out. I expect you've got important homework to do,' he smiled, raising an eyebrow in Mum's direction.

'Would you really go, Dad, for two whole hours?'

'Fancy it, Sheila?'

'Why not. It'll make a nice change. We can have a bite to eat in the pub. In fact, don't expect us home too early, love. We might make an evening of it.'

'The sacrifices you two make for me,' Paul sighed, shaking his head.

'Don't mention it, son,' his dad said gravely.

At Anthony's house Paul resisted all offers of food until they achieved level 40.

'We're going to starve at this rate,' Anthony said, stabbing buttons furiously to evade alien weaponry which was now flicking so fast across the screen that a blink was enough to wipe you out.

'Oh no!' Paul groaned, as his craft plummeted in a blaze of laser fire on level 27.

'We're going backwards,' Anthony cried. 'Right that's it – we're stopping for sustenance. We must be low on blood sugar, that's the problem.'

'You *are* joking. We're just short on practice and in the meantime, Alan and Scott have sailed into the lead.'

'Sailing! You never said anything about that – I can't even swim.'

'Ha ha. I wish you'd take this a bit more seriously.'

'I am, I've fixed up a job at the newsagent's in Fore Street. They want someone every Saturday, paying £2.50 an hour.'

'Great,' Paul said glumly. 'I'm glad to hear you're so confident.'

'Realistic, mate. Thanks to your choice of challenges we're dead meat and I'm going to make sure I've got the cash to pay up before I get my head beaten in by your mates.'

'They're not my mates, at least not any more.'

'Well, they were. Goodness knows how you came to get involved with them in the first place.'

'Oh shut up. Come on, we've got to keep going. You may have a job fixed up but I haven't so I'd appreciate it if you made an effort to help us win, even if it is a pretty tall order.'

Anthony returned to the screen and they made a determined effort but somehow their reactions weren't quick enough and the magical level 30 door eluded them. Paul even managed to shoot Anthony down with a badly timed counter-attack. He was ready to sling the thing through the nearest window when Anthony's father knocked on the door. He was always very formal and slightly overbearing in the way he stared down from his six-foot-odd height. It made Paul grateful for his own dad's easy-going manners even if his flippancy and clowning around was annoying at times.

'Shouldn't you be getting home, Paul? he said, consulting his smart gold watch.

'Yes, Mr Ahmed. Just going.'

'Good luck for tomorrow.'

'Oh, thanks. Actually, we're going to need it. We're stuck on this level,' Paul said, flipping the program off with a scowl.

'Hang on, I've got some inside information for you two. I was speaking to a colleague at work. The way to get into level 38 involves a dummy move, then a double-back to pick up extra weapons and fuel, using these keys, you see?'

Paul was too disillusioned to take much notice. Stuck on level 28 again, he had no real hope of needing Mr Ahmed's valuable tips. Alan would probably give his right arm to know. Anthony, however, was suddenly all fired up again and barely heard Paul's goodbyes as he returned to the screen with renewed enthusiasm, stabbing buttons like a dervish.

Wednesday arrived, dull and threatening rain. School buzzed with anticipation and a couple of teachers moodily commented on how much work was being lost due to these stupid contests and how it was about time Mr Staines put his foot down. Paul was in trouble again, this time for not handing in History homework. He thought for one panic-stricken moment that he'd be put in lunch time detention but escaped with another referral form and a sharp earache session from Miss Nelson. Everyone called her Hardy for obvious reasons but she had the least ability to laugh at anything of any teacher in the school.

Paul was dreading report time, imminent any week now. His mother was going to be off her trolley when she counted all the misconduct referrals he'd accumulated this term. And none of them were his fault – well not directly. How could a person be expected to learn the American Independence Treaty when one's own personal liberties were under such dire threat? Didn't old Hardy realise that?

Scott clapped him on the shoulder in a really friendly way as he informed him, on the way to lunch, that they were on level 37. Was it worth the humiliation of even turning up for the contest? Paul wondered. He hadn't even seen Anthony yet, and wasn't in any great hurry to find out what pitiful level he'd achieved last night. It was pretty depressing to find out that you were a complete duffer at everything – even the things you thought you were good at!

A reluctant sense of fair play somehow guided Paul to the computer room at the allotted time. Groups of Year 9 kids made way for him as he approached the keyboard. He felt like a condemned man. The game had been loaded onto two machines placed strategically opposite each other so that spectators could watch but he and Anthony would have their backs to the other two. Anthony gave him a wink as he sat down and made a thumbs up sign but Paul was sure he was just bluffing for the sake of the other two. From the bags under his eyes, it had been a long night. Was that a good sign or not?

Mr Campbell got the room quiet and the tension was almost tangible. This was a lot more serious than running. Everyone had known Scott would win that but this was a bit different, at least as far as the spectators were concerned.

'Now, we've only got forty minutes and I know you lot play these games for hours on end. However, I'm not going to go brain-dead along with you, so it's a forty minute game, highest level wins. We'll assume a level 32 start because I know it's all pretty tame stuff below that and you're all capable of bettering that. Let's see if anyone can get through the 38 which, I'm told, is the one to sort the men from the boys. Okay, off you go!'

Paul couldn't believe his ears. It was just as well they could leave the level 20s behind, but based on last night's performance they were going to spend forty excruciatingly embarrassing minutes on level 32 while Scott and Alan stormed away.

'Are you watching or am I playing on my own here?' Anthony hissed, as his craft narrowly missed immediate evaporation at the hands of the alien craft.

'Sorry.'

Paul's head spun as the flight simulation program hurled them around a 3D universe populated by legions of hostile craft, meteors and sudden unpredictable black holes. He was vaguely aware of shouts of encouragement or gasps of terror as he narrowly avoided the various obstacles on the path to the hidden, treasure-laden planet. Beside him, Anthony was concentrating hard. A faint gleam of sweat shone over his forehead making the skin glow. His nimble brown fingers flew over the keyboard while his craft gyrated on the screen like a ballet dancer, spinning and pirouetting out of harm's way while their score clocked steadily towards level 36.

Paul was an also-ran, merely an observer of Anthony's brilliance. Paul instinctively knew that they were in the lead from the almost reverential hush which surrounded their PC. A bubble of excitement began to swell in his stomach. He darted a glance at

116

the clock, only ten minutes to go. Anthony had cracked it. Somehow or other he had mastered the crucial moves and, with less than three minutes to go he was on level 38 and performing the complicated back-tracking sequence which shot them onto level 39 and beyond.

A great roar swelled behind them – it was all over. Alan and Scott couldn't touch them, and they knew it. Amid whoops and whistles Mr Campbell called time and announced Anthony and Paul the clear winners by three levels. They were drawn, with the pool game and cycling left. Against all odds, they were still in with a chance.

Anthony was surrounded. Even Scott came over to congratulate him and to find out what the crucial moves had been. To top it all, Karen stalked across and planted a kiss on Anthony's cheek. Several of the girls screamed and giggled but he just sat there, heroic and calm amid all the adulation. He had made it. He was part of the year, one of the lads. Paul felt a twinge of envy. It seemed, after all his efforts, that Anthony had always been able to manage on his own, had not really needed him. Alan sat back behind his PC, dejected and alone. Paul stole a glance in his direction and wondered what he was feeling. One thing was for sure – he had never in his wildest dreams anticipated losing and never imagined that his gang might lean towards the outsider. They were all over Anthony, patting him on the shoulder, nudging him, listening in awe to his modest declarations.

For a moment, Paul met Alan's gaze. He half-smiled in the hope, however distant, that Alan could forget all this stupid rivalry and give in but the other boy's cold, ruthless stare convinced him that nothing had been resolved. Alan was just as determined not to yield, and more persuaded than ever that Paul was his enemy and the cause of the gang's break up. He flung out of his seat, shouldering a way out of the room through the knots of kids. The rest of the gang didn't even notice his departure.

'When's the pool game, Sir?' Karen demanded.

'Tomorrow lunch time, in the sixth form common room. I've managed to persuade them to let us use it for our contest but don't start thinking it'll be a regular event. They're rather jealous of their privileges. However, don't forget the cycle race tonight. You must have permission, written please, from your parents if you want to come along. We'll see them off at six-thirty and I've enlisted the help of a couple of colleagues to be stewards along the route.'

'How far is it, Sir?' another boy asked.

'Six miles in all, across a variety of terrain.'

'My brother says it's dead wet at the moment.' another kid blurted out.

'Old clothes then.' Mr Campbell advised. 'Right you lot, registration in five minutes and I don't want any lates. I've had enough complaints today from teachers telling me you've all been as high as kites. I'll be glad when the whole thing is over and we can get back to normal.'

'Ah, Sir!' There were various groans and protests around the room as kids reluctantly spilled out into the corridor. In fact, the tutor group had rarely taken so much interest in anything or been so keen to turn up to such events.

Paul followed Anthony who was still surrounded by his gaggle of admirers and of course, Karen. He wasn't looking forward to the cycle race really, mainly because he hadn't had much time to get his bike ready and it wasn't up to the mark. Apart from that though, he was beginning to think there wasn't much point in tearing around the moor, breaking a leg or worse when the object of the contest had already been achieved. Anthony didn't have to prove himself any more. He had Karen Schofield on his case and that was more or less proof against anyone!

Even Alan wouldn't mess with Karen. She had a way of crushing you from a distance with one flash of those green eyes and a toss of her glossy brown curls. Every boy in the year had secretly admired or had a crush on her since Year 7 and no one had got anywhere. Now, at the drop of a hat, she was making eyes at Anthony and laughing at his jokes as if they'd been mates since play-school. That must really infuriate Alan. If he wasn't careful, *he'd* end up the outsider, which would serve him right. Still, Paul wasn't much into revenge these days, in spite of everything. He only wished they could all get on with each other and he could start concentrating on more important things than these contests and avoiding teachers or, worse still, kids in the upper school. Getting round school these days was like trying to be the invisible man. Round every corner there was a new danger. It was a good thing he had nerves of steel or he'd be a jabbering wreck by now.

When Mum volunteered to come and watch him cycle, Paul put his foot down with as much tact as he could muster.

'You'd be bored, Mum. There's nothing to see once we get on our way.'

'Well, I could stand on the finishing line and cheer you home.'

'I think you'll be cheering Alan and Scott home, Mum.'

'That's typical of your modesty, love. Still, if you don't want me there...'

Why did parents have to load the guilt on? Paul sighed and capitulated. 'All right, Mum. See you there, then. I think the course takes about three quarters of an hour.' Well it would if you had a half-decent bike. He'd be hobbling in with his battered body somewhere around eight o'clock.

Anthony was in high spirits when Paul called for him a little after half past five that evening. He was sporting a yellow jumper and a cocky smile.

'You're hopeful, aren't you?' Paul commented.

'Got to be confident, mate. With any luck, I won't even have to start that job. I might do it anyway, though, on second thoughts. I need the cash to take Karen out next Saturday evening.'

'That was quick work!' Paul said drily.

'It's how you chat 'em up, mate.'

'You couldn't chat up my Granny – she's just feeling sorry for you. She'll dump you, before you know it.'

'You're jealous, mate.'

Paul looked up and smiled at him. It was nice to know he wasn't being cast aside at the first suggestion of something more interesting.

'I might ask that Jane. We'd make a foursome then.' The words surprised Paul even as he spoke them. He just might do it though.

'All set then?' Anthony said.

'No problem,' Paul muttered sarcastically.

'I don't care any more, really.'

'I know what you mean.'

'Do you reckon Alan'll really make us pay up if we lose.'

'Why, would you refuse?'

'I might. Well, he's nothing, is he? Scott and Kevin said he's a load of hot air.'

'I suppose he is.' Paul surprised himself saying that as well. Mind you, it did seem less threatening now, taking the gang on. They weren't a gang for one thing and Alan wasn't a real leader any more. Paul could almost feel a twinge of pity, until he remembered that cold stare. He knew Alan would try anything to get back at him. He was determined to keep well ahead or behind him on the course and avoid any accidental collisions.

'Rain, that's all we need!' Anthony groaned, wrinkling his nose at the sky as several large droplets fell as heavy as hail on his head. They hung in the dense curls like jewels.

The group of supporters was pretty thin. Only a few stoic friends had turned up. Mr Campbell had an orange cagoule on. Paul wished he'd thought to bring one and looked around hopefully for his mum and the car but she wasn't there. He regretted his disparaging remarks to her. They always had waterproofs in the boot.

Alan was there with his super de-luxe 25 gear job and his go-faster cycling shorts. Mr Campbell had insisted on them wearing cycling helmets and Paul's chin strap was sawing his skin uncomfortably in the wet. He thought about releasing it and padding it somehow but suddenly they were being lined up and there was no time. They rolled up to the start, the whistle blew and they were off.

Anthony kicked off well and Paul ate his mud as he sloshed through a puddle, sending a wake of red slop up into the air. Paul wished mud guards weren't so un-cool these days as he felt dirty water spraying up his back. Scott was tucked behind him and they jostled for position for a while. Anthony was hard on Alan's tail, keeping a lot closer than Paul thought he would. Those gangly legs and arms were somehow more co-ordinated and pedalling like fury up a one-in-four hill.

In places, the cinder track provided a well-drained if bumpy surface. Paul understood what wishbone suspension might mean as his old bone-shaker rattled across the pebbles with teeth-juddering urgency. It was more than he could manage to keep on an even keel as his front wheel kept sliding away from him. Legs straining, he hauled himself up the slope and slid crab-wise down the other side straight into a ditch at the bottom. Scott, hard on his tail, skidded into him and both boys lay panting in the slime.

Various crude expletives were exchanged in a fairly friendly manner and they dragged themselves out of the mire and untangled their bikes.

'Whose stupid idea was this?' Scott shouted, as his trainer was sucked off his left foot. Paul bent down and hooked it out, lobbing it across to the other boy.

'Ta. We're still gonna thrash you,' he laughed, climbing aboard.

'Dream on,' Paul returned, ignoring the flapping of his muddy shirt, cold and heavy against his skin.

As wet as they were, both boys threw themselves into the race with renewed vigour. They passed Mr Parr and realised they were two miles into the course. Alan and Anthony were way ahead but occasionally

Paul got a glimpse of the yellow jumper flashing in a blur through the trees. It gave him new heart.

He tucked his head down, bunny-hopped a series of logs and found himself surprisingly close to Scott as they emerged onto the open track again. A couple of hair-pin bends nearly had Paul off but he refused to let nerves slow him down. With a whoop of success, he passed Scott again and free-wheeled ludicrously down another mud bank. Over to his right he glimpsed the canal basin and tow-path. The course cut close to it at this point. He was aware of something else too, the group of bikes on the road parallel to them, that kid in front with the air rifle slung over his shoulder.

Instinctively he flung his front wheel sideways and slowed to a gravel-splintering stop. Scott, closing rapidly nearly upended as he was forced to apply the brakes.

'What do think you're playing at?' he said fiercely, shaking his head to clear the water out of his eyes. 'That kid, look. It's him. The one who shoots the swans.' The words came out in stifled sobs as Paul tried to get his breath. 'I'm going after them.'

'What about the race?'

'Forget the race. Get the others!' Paul screamed over his shoulder, as he pedalled away furiously towards the road and the canal. He wasn't even sure if Scott had heard him or whether he'd do as he asked. It didn't matter – he was going after them, on his own, if necessary.

Paul veered off the track towards the road, crashing through bracken which plucked at his bare legs and became entwined in the spokes of his wheels. He braced himself for the inevitable plunge down the last bank before his front wheel hit the road, sending a judder up his arms which carried on into his neck and set his teeth chattering.

An age later, or so it seemed, his back wheel made contact with the road and he was able to steer properly, although something was wrong with his front fork which made it hard to steer straight without this awful rasping metallic sound. He'd twisted the frame, most likely, but it couldn't be helped.

Legs straining, Paul thundered on up the road, tailing the last bike in the gaggle of kids he'd spotted from higher up. There was no time to feel frightened or to plan what he would do if he managed to catch them. Panic and adrenaline surged new power through his limbs and he pedalled harder.

Round the next bend he had them in sight and controlled his speed accordingly. There was no point in careering straight through the centre of them. He recognised the two older kids in front and kept his face down. His vision was blurred with sweat and his eyes stung with the salt. There were six of them, the two leaders both carried air rifles, slung over their backs by wide leather straps. They had to be planning trouble for the swans and this time he was going to thwart them. Whatever it took, he'd make sure they didn't get to their targets.

Fear melted for a moment in the face of this overwhelming determination and Paul experienced a kind of weird confidence which calmed his erratic breathing and enabled him to think straight for a moment. He couldn't take them all on himself. It wasn't a matter of being scared to fight. He could have taken all six of them on, one after the other but it wouldn't be like that. If they bundled him together, he didn't stand a chance. No, it had to be brain-work. Follow them, then don't attract attention. The warden might be down there. No, he'd needed volunteers this week. Mum and Dad had done it last night. Who might be there tonight? No way of knowing. The police then. Too far to cycle into town. He didn't dare let them out of his sight. A telephone box – he could phone 999. No good, there were no phone boxes round here. Stop wasting time – think!

The group slowed down, dismounted from their bikes and left them in a heap near the lock gates. Paul pedalled so slowly he nearly toppled off. What should he do? They were lounging about, messing around and shoving each other. Paul stood up in the saddle, kept his face well down and cycled strongly towards them. His heart pounded again, so loudly he imagined the group would hear it as he passed them.

Paul heard the jeering comments as he cycled by them.

'Hey, look at that!'

'Came out of the swamp. It's primeval.'

'Yeah, and the bike!'

The younger lads exploded into fits of giggles. Someone picked up a stone and lobbed it in Paul's direction. It glanced off his shoulder and he was too absorbed in his thoughts to notice the dull pain. He cycled well out of distance before prodding the ground with his left toe to slow the bike. Paul swung his leg over and lowered his bike gently into the wet grass beside the towpath. He stood helplessly for a moment, unsure whether to double-back and keep the yobs under observation or go on and try to warn whoever was guarding the nest. Trouble was, the young cygnets were feeding independently now and the group swam at least a mile or so from the nest either way up the canal. He'd have to tail the yobs if he wanted to be sure they weren't up to no good.

He knelt in the long grass for a moment and fiddled with the chin strap of his helmet. It was a relief to get it off. He slung it next to his bike and ran dirty fingers through his plastered-down hair. Paul was aware of the mud hardening on his skin, pulling his cheeks as he tried to move his mouth. Shivering with cold, he got to his feet and stooped awkwardly as he edged along the tow-path back towards the group. He could hear their raucous voices which helped in judging their distance. If only the others were here, someone could go and get help. It wouldn't be so agonising wondering what to do for the best.

The voices became hushed, then silent altogether. Where were they? What were they doing? In a panic, Paul straightened and started trotting towards where he's last seen them. He burst into the clearing by the locks to discover them gone, along with their bikes.

Cursing himself, Paul began to jog. How could he have lost them? Why hadn't he hung back rather than carried on past them? He ought to go back and get his own bike. No, it was too late for that – he'd lose them completely. Rage at his own incompetence and at the yobs' evil intentions filled his head and sent sparks exploding in his brain. He floundered along the path on foot like a drowning man wading through weeds, oblivious to the nettles brushing maliciously against his legs and arms. At this rate he'd be scarred for life or his skin would be hanging off in ribbons.

A few nettles suddenly didn't seem so important, however, as he stumbled almost literally upon the bikes discarded in a heap in his path. He was relieved and afraid all at once. At least he must be close to them but maybe they'd seen something, the swans, to make them take to their feet again. Straining to hear their voices, Paul heard nothing for a minute, which seemed like an hour, and then the ear-splitting shot rang out and the sound penetrated his brain and seemed to hang there like a lead weight.

'No!' The scream was all around him and inside his head before Paul realised *he* was making the sound. He plunged towards the direction of the shot and saw the yobs hurling stones and broken branches into the canal. The swans were just beyond them, their usually graceful progress a ragged, ungainly crashing and flapping of wings and webbed feet. The cygnets couldn't fly yet and the female wouldn't leave them but she arched her enormous wing span and hissed heroically in the face of the jeering onslaught. Paul couldn't see whether the shot had injured any of them but one of the older boys was lining up to take a second aim. He had the female in his sights and in easy range as Paul pushed a hand in someone's face, shook off a rugby-tackle hold from one of the smaller kids and launched himself onto the back of the boy aiming at the swan. He held on round his neck as the boy spluttered and swore, trying to keep his balance and throw Paul off at the same time.

Legs dangling, Paul felt himself being spun round like a piece of washing on a line. The canal lurched drunkenly in and out of his view and his fingers started to slip in the shiny material of the older boy's jacket. Still he clung on and yelled for all he was worth, until the thwack of something very hard and solid landed round his left ear and he dropped to the ground like a swatted fly.

What would have happened next, Paul didn't like to think. Much later, he remembered the butt of the rifle being raised to club him again this time full in the face before chaos broke loose and his assailants were scattered by the arrival of Alan, Scott and Anthony on their bikes, flying into the middle of everything.

Paul raised his head and half-rolled away from the mass bundle of flying fists and kicking feet. Something warm and sticky was running down his neck and he felt woozy as if in a half-daze. Vaguely aware of a struggle going on all around him, Paul could only lie on the ground, winded, and wait for it all to end. For the life of him, he couldn't have got up.

'Break it up, the lot of you!' A deep male voice boomed over the noises of the skirmish. It was joined by several others, crashing through the undergrowth.

Someone dropped to their knees beside Paul and peered anxiously into his eyes.

'Ugh!' he groaned, writhing.

'What is it?' Alan said leaning over him in consternation. 'Are you all right? Are you in pain?'

'Yes, you idiot, you're kneeling on my hand!' Paul hissed through clenched teeth.

'Sorry mate! I thought you were dead or something.' Alan shifted his knee. His brow was still wrinkled with concern. Paul was giddy but he felt like giggling. Alan's face was so comical close up, his concern so ironic.

'You've got all blood in your ear,' Alan said.

'You've got blood on your nose,' Paul returned.

'Have I? Oh, yes!' Alan's face broke into a wide smile as he fingered his sore nose tentatively. 'I didn't half give that kid a smack.'

'Which one?'

'The one who clobbered you.'

'Thanks.'

'No problem, mate.'

Paul smiled weakly at the familiar friendly tone, before he remembered the swans. His face creased again. 'Did they hurt them?' he said, gripping Alan's arm urgently.

'It's all right. They swam away.'

'All of them – you're sure?'

'Certain.'

'Give him some air there,' the male voice said.

Paul recognised the game warden's tanned features. 'You've taken a nasty knock there, lad. Don't move. The police are calling an ambulance and they should be here any moment.'

'I'm all right now,' Paul protested, but he felt a bit sick all of a sudden and his ear was throbbing something awful.

'Nobody move. I'm going to want statements from all of you once we've contacted your parents,' one of the policemen said. Paul wondered how many more people were going to turn up.

It wasn't long before two ambulance men arrived with a wheelchair which they somehow negotiated along the tow-path with him strapped into it and swathed in blankets, a temporary dressing having been wound around his head. Paul's mum was waiting in the car park with Mr Campbell and Paul thought she was going to faint when she saw him.

'What on earth... ?'

'Would you like to come with us in the ambulance?' one of the men asked.

'Yes of course. Oh Paul, how could you?' she scolded, for all the world as if he'd purposely got himself into that state.

'My bike,' he suddenly remembered.

'Oh be quiet!' mum said crossly, 'as if that matters now!' Then she bent down and hugged him, squeezing his battered ear all over again.

'We'll look after your bike,' Anthony called after him as the doors of the ambulance closed on Paul and his mum. The last view Paul had was of Anthony's brown face between Scott's and Alan's, all so mud-streaked and blooded that they looked the same colour. He smiled faintly to himself before allowing his head to relax into the cool pillow that someone had tucked behind it.

It was two days later before Paul saw anybody. He'd had a thorough check-up at the hospital, including an X-ray because the bump behind his ear, so Mum informed him, had been spectacular even by the standards of the casualty ward. He'd been threatened with an overnight stay in hospital but the doctor had relented when the X-ray came back clear. Paul secretly thought the doctor *may* have been influenced by his mum asking if she could stay the night as well. That might have been enough to send all his staff crazy, the way she was going on.

Finally back home, she hadn't stopped asking him how he felt, putting her hand on his brow as if he might have developed a temperature and generally giving him even more ear-ache than he already had by refusing to stop her nagging.

'For goodness' sake, woman, give the boy some peace,' Dad said eventually.

'Well, that's easy for you to say. You're not the one who had to sit in the ambulance with him, wondering whether he'd fractured his skull or not.'

Paul exchanged a sympathetic glance with his dad. He was in for it now.

'When can I get back to school, Mum?'

'You're in no fit state for school,' she snapped.

Paul sighed. Was this the woman who never allowed him to stay off school even when he was struck down by plague and consumption?

'He's only had a knock on the head, love,' Dad soothed, lowering his newspaper.

'I'd like to give him another one for all the trouble he's caused,' she returned, snatching up Paul's empty glass and retreating to the kitchen.

'What's got into *her*?' Paul grumbled as he flicked

through the television channels idly, finding nothing worth watching.

'She was worried about you,' Dad said, shaking out his newspaper, 'and a bit annoyed you'd gone fighting again.'

'Anybody would think I *liked* getting smacked round the ear. I've never been so terrified in my life as I was when I saw those yobs.'

'You didn't run away though.'

'I couldn't. They'd have killed the swans.'

'I know and we're very proud of you.'

'Mum thinks I was stupid.'

'No she doesn't. Well, yes she *does* of course, but you did exactly what she'd have expected you to do.'

Paul raised a quizzical eyebrow at his dad, who simply winked back and then put his attention to the article he'd attempted to read for about half a dozen times now. Paul felt the lump behind his ear tentatively. It had gone down a lot but still felt sore.

Trouble was, there wasn't any pleasure in being off school if he couldn't go out, and he was missing Anthony and his daft ways. Glancing out of the window he grinned again at the sight of their demolished hedge. Even with Dad's remedial efforts at tidying up, it still looked pretty wonky. And then walking past the hedge, as if on cue, came the idiot responsible. Paul had never been more pleased to see anyone. He was at the door before Anthony had time to ring the bell.

'Watcha.'

'How are you feeling?'

'Okay.'

There was a kind of shyness between them after the gap of two days. It wasn't the time lapse so much as the situation which had changed. They sat awkwardly in Paul's room not quite knowing what to say to each other.

'How's school?' Paul asked.

'Oh great. It's totally different now – with the gang, I mean.'

'Oh.' Paul felt glad yet, at the same time, a twinge of jealously crept in. Anthony was a part of the gang, just like that, and he was stuck at home, out of it all.

'Alan wants to see you,' Anthony murmured, dead serious.

'Oh yes.' Paul felt the hair rise on his neck.

'Says you owe him, seeing as how you dropped out of the contest.'

Paul's jaw nearly hit the floor. 'Cheeky swine! I've a good mind to...' Paul stopped as Anthony rolled over on the bed in fits of laughter.

'Very funny,' he said, realising he'd been had.

'You should have seen your face!' Anthony said.

'Shut up, you idiot. I knew you were messing about.'

'You looked scared to death.'

Paul thumped him soundly in the back.

'Go on – admit it – you thought I was being serious.'

'Course I didn't,' Paul returned huffily.

'Mind you, you did drop out of the contest, didn't you?'

'I'll drop on you in a minute,' Paul scowled.

'I think that bump on the head's affected you, mate. Knocked out your sense of humour. Anyway, when are you being released?'

'How did you guess?'

'I've phoned you loads of times and your mum kept telling me you were asleep, so I knew you were under lock and key. Well, tomorrow you've *got* to get out because the warden's taking us to the swan sanctuary.'

'Why?'

'To get the male. He said we could help release him back on the canal.'

'I'm not missing that,' Paul vowed, swinging himself off the bed.

'Where are you going?'

'I've got to start bargaining for parole with her downstairs.'

It was a beautiful evening just as the heat of the sun mellowed and the canal hummed with clouds of insects hovering over its tranquil surface. A dragonfly dipped and rose over a clump of rushes and the voices of children playing in the park floated across on the gentle breeze. The game warden paused to drink in the atmosphere for a while before turning to open up the back of the van.

The four boys controlled their desire to crowd round the crate for fear of further disturbing its disgruntled occupant. It had taken three volunteers at the swan sanctuary nearly an hour to corner and capture him which was some proof of how quickly and successfully he had healed. Now, effectively straight-jacketed in a hessian bag and then crated, his ferocious power had been turned into a hissing but helpless bundle of irritation.

During the capture, the boys had been treated like guests of honour, touring the lake where hundreds of swans swam in vast white clouds across the water. The tour of cages and pens housing sick or injured birds had been fascinating but sad. So many of the injuries, it seemed to the boys, were the direct result of people being careless or downright cruel. At least a dozen birds had had fishing hooks and line in their throat or around their feet, while several others had been poisoned by people dumping rubbish in and around their habitat.

The sanctuary was vast and, in its own way, a beautiful place, but here on the canal was where Paul thought *his* swans fitted best. Funnily enough, Alan and Scott had been absorbed in asking questions and never left the warden's side at the sanctuary. They volunteered to hold the crate and carried it as gingerly as if it contained the crown jewels, down to the water's edge.

'Here will do, boys. Set him down and then stand back. When I let him go, he's just as likely to turn around and let us know exactly what he thinks of us.'

'His mate's not here, though,' Anthony said, peering up and down the canal anxiously.

'She'll turn up.'

'Yeah, typical of a woman to be late!' Scott said.

'She's there, look!' Paul said, pointing through the reeds which choked one section of the canal where an overflow channel had been built. The water was very shallow there and, presumably, a rich feeding ground. Very often the family of swans went there to dabble their beaks in the weedy mud. She swam, head erect, unperturbed by the calamity which had befallen her nesting season that year, followed by the four cygnets, now nearly as large as her but still the dusky brown colour of juveniles. Unexpectedly, she parted her beak and honked insistently in their direction. Did she know he was there?

At the noise, the wrestling from within the box reached fever pitch. The warden slid the heavy bolt

135

and picked up the hessian bag by its sturdy handles. With strong, deft fingers he undid the row of buckles, whipped off the cloth and the swan was spilled out onto the grassy bank. His long neck snaked maliciously at the warden's leg but the sudden urgent honking from across the canal distracted him. With a disgusted shake of feathers and a waddling gait on unsteady feet, he reached the edge, plopped noisily into the canal and became transformed into an elegant schooner, cutting water like a hot knife through butter.

The boys and the man stood in respectful silence as he cruised towards his mate and she set up a honking welcome. The cygnets crowded round, uncertain at first about the intruder and then as effusive as the female. They swam off together and were soon calmly feeding as if nothing had ever interrupted their quiet existence.

'Fantastic,' Alan said, his eyes glowing with pleasure as he watched the group.

Paul was surprised. He'd never imagined Alan getting a kick out of this kind of experience.

'I must be getting off,' the warden said, tidying up in a very matter of fact way, as if it was all in a day's work rather than the best thing to experience in a whole lifetime, which was how Paul felt. A sudden wave of paternal anxiety swept over him.

'I almost wish they were all at the sanctuary,' Paul blurted out.

The warden nodded understandingly. 'I know what you mean. It's hard to set them off and wonder what's in store for them next but they're wild and free, and they deserve to be. We can't put a round-the-clock guard on them. They'll just have to take their chances, the same as everything in this world. You lot have done your best, and no one can do more.'

'It's been a great afternoon,' Alan said.

'Glad you enjoyed it. Perhaps I'll see you around.'

'Definitely,' they all chorused.

'Don't worry too much, Paul,' the man added kindly, seeing his sad face. 'Those boys are in so much trouble with the police and the RSPB, who are prosecuting with proper evidence this time. I don't think they'll be showing their faces down this way again for a very long time.'

They watched the warden pack his van, and exchanged a few more words before he drove off, swirling a fine layer of dust about their feet.

'Cracking couple of days,' Scott said, rubbing his hands together.

'Well, it was for Paul,' Anthony teased.

'I wish I'd got there first,' Alan said, 'I'd have had him spitting out his own teeth.'

Paul raised his eyes but said nothing. Alan couldn't help being the way he was.

'What about the contest then?' Paul said.

'Oh that!' Alan said dismissively.

'Who won?'

'The cycling you mean? Well, *we* did, didn't we, Scott?'

'What, oh yeah, on account of Paul taking a wrong turn! Leaving the course was against the rules.'

'I was leading all the way,' Anthony protested.

'You never were.'

'I *would* have been, though, if you'd fallen off or something!' Anthony grinned.

'Mr Staines made Campbell call it off after the cycling. He said the whole thing had got out of hand

and he wasn't willing to risk the school's good name – something like that,' Scott explained.

'Mind you,' Anthony put in, 'that didn't stop him contacting the newspaper and saying the sponsorship thing had been his idea. I suppose it was better publicity than seeing your battered face in the papers,' he added.

'We collected £120 altogether. Mr Campbell let us vote for two charities and in the end we chose two, the children's hospital and the swan sanctuary. That Jane kept voting twice and saying she was using your vote, Paul, because she knew what you'd have wanted.' Scott paused for breath, then added thoughtfully. 'She made a get well card for you too and we all had to sign it.'

'She *made* it?' Paul said, remembering the card, covered in flowers and pictures of grapes which he'd tossed under a load of other papers on his desk.

'Anyone would think she had a thing about you,' Scott rambled on.

Paul blushed, made a mental note to get the card back on his bedside table for a closer look, then changed the direction of the conversation.

'Is it really all off then, the contest?'

'Yeah,' Alan said, embarrassed, as if he didn't want to be reminded about it. 'Mr Campbell declared it a draw.'

'And after all that pool practice,' Anthony sighed. 'We'd have walked all over you.'

'Well if that's how you feel...' Scott said.

'No thanks, we'll accept the draw, if it's all the same to everyone,' Paul interrupted, before Alan got on his high horse again. Alan was off on another tack though.

'That bike of yours is crummy,' he said. 'We were well embarrassed, wheeling it back to your place.'

'I think it's had it. I twisted the front forks and Dad says it's not worth trying to repair,' Paul replied.

'Good, you can get something decent then.'

At one time Paul would have been thrown into a panic wondering how much he could make his parents spend on a bike, knowing it would have to have the latest this, that or other to be worth considering. Now, he didn't care so much. It didn't matter what Alan thought, so he was under no pressure. The relief of this struck Paul with an almost tangible force.

'I'll probably look in the papers for something second-hand,' he heard himself saying calmly.

Alan looked shocked and opened his mouth to make a cutting retort and then shut it again. He half-looked at Paul out of the corner of his eye and something about the other boy's confident stride and the set of his chin made him back off. He couldn't mess with him any more; he was his own boss.

'I might be selling mine later this year. Dad's getting me the new model,' he volunteered.

Paul smiled at him and took the olive branch. 'Great – let me know when. I'd like first refusal – it's a brilliant bike.' He just added that last comment on the spur of the moment, not to be creepy or anything but to show there were no hard feelings. He didn't think he could ever be really good mates with Alan again, but who knew? Alan was changing. For a start he was here, being concerned about something other than himself, talking to Anthony like a human being. At this rate he could turn into a really decent person if he didn't watch it.

A little further on, they parted company, Scott and Alan going back into town, Anthony and Paul crossing the footbridge which eventually led back to their estate.

'Show me that computer game tomorrow,' Alan called to Anthony over his shoulder.

'Yeah, okay.'

He and Paul slouched against the footbridge and watched the swans for one last time before turning for home. There was a companionable silence which neither seemed keen to break. At last Anthony spoke.

'What are you thinking about?'

'Something Campbell said to me a bit ago.'

'What?'

'Nothing, really. I was going on about praying and how things didn't happen as they should. I was just thinking how things couldn't have turned out much better, after a load of misery on the way! I was just wondering whether God *did* have a sort of plan in mind when he lumbered me with you, after all.'

'You took a heck of a lot of flak this term because of me,' Anthony said quietly.

'It was because of *me* in the end,' Paul said. 'Alan had to change, but so did I. You coming on the scene was the catalyst to get it started, that's all. I used to think friends were the most important thing in my life.'

'Aren't they?'

'In one way, but now there's other things to consider, and doing what you believe is right is one of them, not just following everyone else because it's easier.'

'I thought you were a bit of a wimp when I first met you,' Anthony confessed.

'Thanks!' Paul's tone was heavily sarcastic.

'No, I was wrong. You're different from my mates back in Birmingham. You can be straight without being wet. Even Alan admires that!'

Paul gave a derisory snort.

'It's true. I tell you what, though, you can stop me playing on arcades, you might even get me to church but we're not turning into a couple of monks. This weekend we're going out on a date – a proper one!'

'No problem,' said Paul, punching Anthony lightly in the arm. 'I've got women queuing up for me.'

It was Anthony's turn to pull a face.

'One of them, anyway! Come on – last one back to my place makes the fish finger sandwiches.'

on line with God

David Lawrence

At last! practical help with how to pray. Plus a **free CD** featuring extracts of worship songs by the World Wide Message Tribe.

Price £5.99
ISBN 1 85999 185 8